FOREST OF THE SASQUATCH II

DEFY THE CONVENANT, FACE THE WRATH

LUKA T. JACOBS

Cover Design, Book Design & Formatting: Luka T. Jacobs.

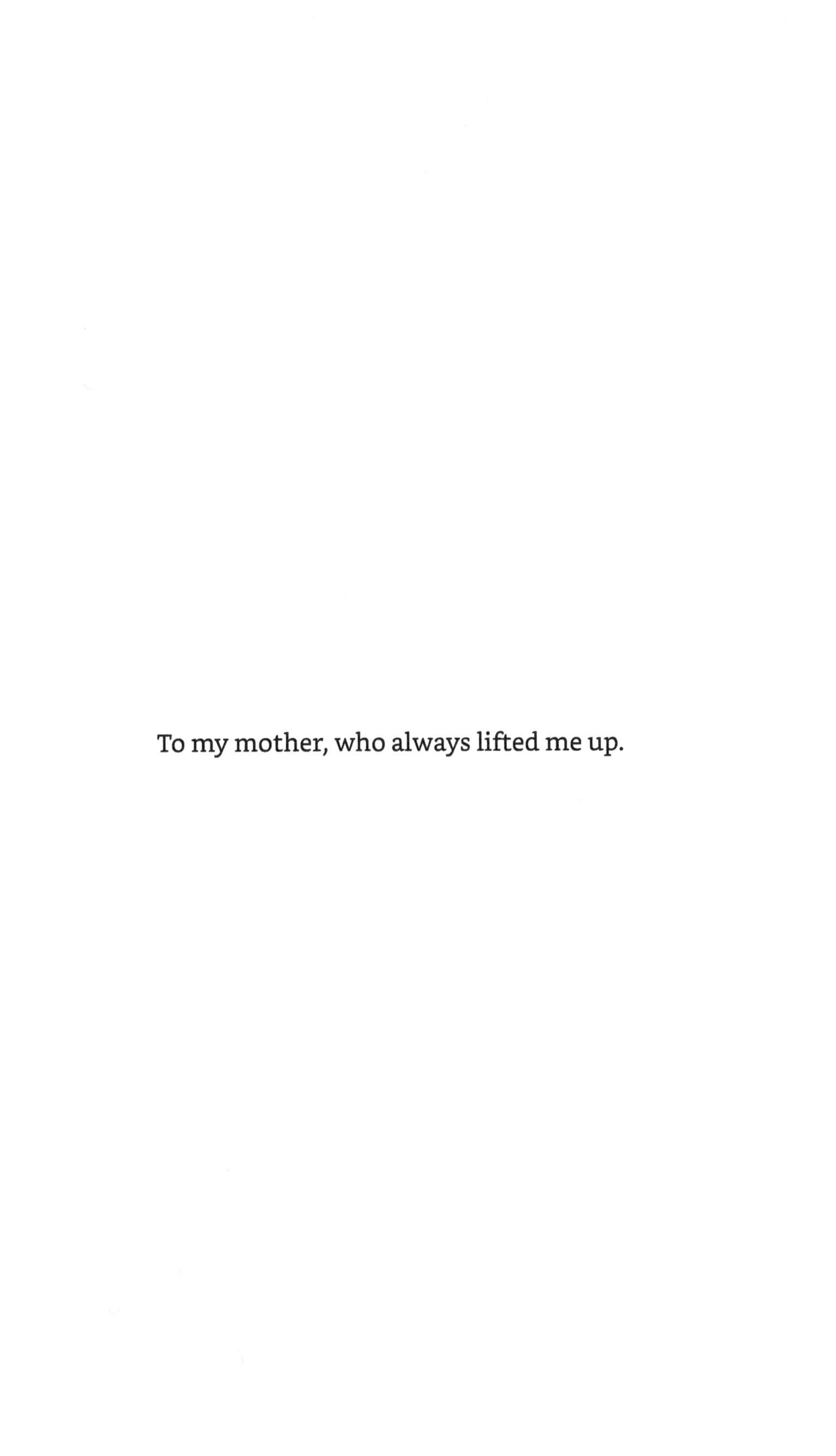

To my mother, who always lifted me up.

FROM THE AUTHOR

Hey there, fearless reader!

First off, thank you for venturing back into the woods with me. *Forest of the Sasquatch II* can stand on its own, but let's be real, would you watch the sequel to a monster movie without seeing the first one? You *could*... but you'd be missing out on all the good stuff that got us here. So if you haven't read *Forest of the Sasquatch* yet, consider this your friendly nudge to start there.

As an indie author, I survive on late-night writing sessions, and, most importantly, your support. Your feedback, reviews and general enthusiasm keep this whole adventure going. Want to chat about the book (or cryptids)? Join me on **Facebook** or through my **newsletter**, I'd love to hear from you!

Hope you enjoy the journey... and if you're going out into the wilds, maybe keep your wits about you. You never know what's lurking in the woods.

Luka T. Jacobs

CONTENTS

PROLOGUE

Aluk stood alone on the edge of the lake. He stared at the calm, black water, only his breath disturbing the surface. The blood on his hands ran down his fingers in slow rivulets, dark against the early light. It trailed into the lake, curling like smoke beneath the surface before fading into nothing.

The hunt had been easy. A young deer, quick and lean, but no match for him. It had not suffered.

Aluk crouched and washed the blood from his hands. The chill of the water bit at his skin, but he welcomed it. He let it sting. It helped him think.

Behind him, the sanctuary waited in silence. It was still early, the sky just beginning to shift from deep black to the color of ash. The rest of the hunting party were already heading back to the cave with their kills. Now the clan lingered in the warmth of the stone, conserving energy, waiting for the feast to begin, especially after the chaos of the day before.

The new one, the hairless male they had captured, still breathed.

Aluk had made sure of it.

He hadn't spoken the reason aloud, not even to the Elder. But somewhere deep inside, he knew why.

The others would come. The hairless ones always came when one of their own was taken. They followed scent, memory, sound. They hunted, too.

So let them.

Let them come.

He would end them all.

He rose to his full height and stared across the water. The lake stretched wide, its far edge hidden in morning shadow. The cold wind tugged at the wet hair along his arms. Somewhere in the dark canopy behind him, a tree creaked softly, the earth adjusting to his weight. But nothing else stirred.

A memory returned as he stood there, solitary, with only his breath, the water and the diminishing smell of blood.

One that never left for long.

He had been young. Barely old enough to move on his own. His arms were thin then, his frame still growing into its strength. His father had taken him into the forest to learn.

They moved without sound, the way all of their kind did. His father walked with purpose. Aluk, still learning the rhythm of his limbs, swung playfully in the lower branches overhead. He remembered the feeling, how free it was, how high the trees had seemed.

Then his world changed.

He had flung himself from a branch onto the dirt, his bare feet soft against the path. He turned, proud of the landing, ready to boast.

But his father's eyes were wide.

Aluk had no time to question it. His father dove forward and shoved him hard in the chest.

Aluk flew backward into the brush just as the loud beast came crashing down the path.

He had never seen anything like it. A giant creature of metal, with flat eyes and howling breath. It rolled over the dirt trail with black legs made of stone. And on its back, it carried the broken corpses of trees, long-dead trunks stripped of skin and stacked like bones.

It struck his father square on.

There had been a sound, something that still woke Aluk in his sleep. A crack, a crunch, and then the deep silence that followed. His father had not cried out. He had only fallen.

Aluk watched, frozen in the thick underbrush, not daring to move. Not blinking.

The machine hissed and groaned as it stopped. A figure stepped out from its side, small and pale. Hairless. It moved slowly, cautiously, stepping toward the still body on the dirt.

Aluk remembered the way the figure looked at his father, then turned and scanned the trees, as if it could feel something watching.

His only movement was a slight tremor, fear holding him immobile. He didn't understand what he was seeing. He only knew that his father didn't move.

Then the figure returned to the beast and climbed inside.

Aluk remained hidden for hours.

The sky shifted above him. Eventually, other machines came, one with flashing lights, colors that made the trees seem wrong. A dark one followed, its form boxy and strange, growling low as it approached.

They used long metal arms to lift his father's body.

They wrapped him in cloth and hid him inside the black beast.

Aluk had watched until the last sound faded. Then he ran.

He ran harder than he ever had, his lungs burning as he crossed ridge and root, leaping over streams, crashing through underbrush until he reached the sanctuary. His mother had found him shaking, unable to speak.

She had known before he said a word.

Aluk never saw his father again.

He had waited for many days afterward, crouched in the trees, watching the trail where it had happened. But his father never came back.

His mother mourned for many seasons until she went into the cave one night and passed into the greater beyond.

And from that day forward, Aluk's heart held only one truth.

They take.

They always take.

Now, so would he.

He stood at the water's edge, letting the memory settle, letting the cold wind fill his chest. His eyes narrowed. He could still picture the face of the one who had looked at his father's body and done nothing. He remembered the color of its skin, the way it walked and the scent of fear and sweat.

The memory carved itself deeper every time he let it come.

From behind him, the faintest rustle.

He turned, but it was only the trees. Shifting. Stretching toward the morning.

He looked down at the water again.

The surface reflected him, broad shoulders, long dark hair that absorbed light, eyes like red breath. He was no longer the child who had seen his father taken away by the hairless ones. He was strength. He was the old ways made new.

The hate burned low, steady.

He understood now why he had spared the hairless one tied to the tree.

It wasn't mercy.

It was a message.

They would come for him. Others always did. And like before, they would bring their thunder sticks. They would try to take what wasn't theirs.

He would show them what it meant to bleed.

There was nothing in this forest that he feared. Even the hairless ones.

CHAPTER 1

The first thing Levi felt was thirst.

His tongue stuck to the roof of his mouth, his throat dry and raw. His body ached. His legs were stiff, his arms burned, and his skin stung from deep scratches.

Levi blinked against the brightness of the overhead lights, trying to focus on the shapes beside him. He felt sluggish and his head felt heavy.

A warm hand gripped his.

"Oh my God, Levi."

His mother.

Pain shot through his neck as he winced, turning his head. Claire Holloway came into view. Worry etched her face, her eyes red-rimmed and her expression strained. Behind her stood his father, David Holloway, arms crossed. His face was unreadable.

"You're awake," Claire whispered. "Thank God."

Levi swallowed, his throat protesting. He was both physically and mentally depleted.

"How long?" His voice came out hoarse.

His mother brushed damp hair from his forehead. The warmth steadied him. "They found you yesterday morning. The helicopter flew you to Duluth. As soon as they landed, the medics put you on a stretcher, and you passed out."

A day.

It came rushing back. The forest. His friends. The screams. The blood. Running until his lungs burned. The monsters that hunted him. The helicopter.

A surge of raw, breathless panic choked him, stealing his breath.

His mother squeezed his hand tighter. "Levi, do you remember what you said?"

Levi blinked at her. "What?"

She glanced behind before continuing. "Right before you passed out. When they put you on the stretcher."

His father exhaled. "You told them your friends were dead."

Levi felt a queasy feeling in his stomach. "They are."

His mother's eyes filled with fresh tears, but something about her expression made his gut sink. It wasn't just sadness. It was uncertainty.

"That's not all you said," his father said.

Levi frowned.

Claire's fingers trembled. "You told them it was Sasquatch. As in Bigfoot."

Silence.

The words sat between them like something rotten.

Levi froze. Had he really said that?

Then he remembered. The moment they found him. Hands grabbing him, lifting him into the helicopter. The questions. Their shock.

But he had said it.

Because it was true.

His pulse picked up. "I didn't imagine it. They were there.

They killed them. They…"

A knock at the door cut him off.

A man in a dark suit stepped inside, another right behind him. Detectives.

"Levi Holloway?" The first detective, Burke, had a gravelly voice, hard eyes and the kind of stare that stripped a man down to his bones. "We need to talk."

His mother frowned. "Now? He just woke up."

Burke ignored her. He pulled a small notebook from his coat. The other detective, Hughes, leaned against the doorframe with arms crossed, watching Levi carefully.

Levi swallowed and tried to sit up. Something about the way they looked at him didn't feel right.

Burke flipped through his notes, then looked Levi in the eye. "Before I ask you anything, I have to read you your rights."

His father stepped forward. "Wait—what? You think he's guilty?"

Burke didn't flinch. "It's procedure. By law, I have to read him his rights before asking any questions."

Frustrated, his father turned away, running a hand through his hair.

Burke recited the rights clearly and without emotion. When he finished, Levi nodded.

"I understand," Levi said quietly. "You can ask whatever you want. I've got nothing to hide."

Then Burke continued, voice flat. "Five men went into the forest with you." He lifted his gaze. "You're the only one who came out."

That sounded like an accusation, Levi thought.

Burke turned a page in his notebook, raising an eyebrow as he spoke. "You told the medics your friends were killed by… 'Sasquatch.'"

Levi didn't answer.

Burke studied him. "That's quite the claim."

Levi's heart pounded.

Burke exhaled, tapping his pen against the notebook. "Why don't you walk us through it? What exactly happened out there?"

Levi glanced at his father, but David wouldn't meet his

eyes. His jaw was clenched so tight Levi thought his teeth might break.

They don't believe me.

Levi exhaled shakily. His chest ached. His mind screamed. But the words sat there like lead on his tongue.

The forest. The Sasquatch. The massacre.

Why would they believe him?

They thought he killed his friends.

As Burke pulled up a chair, fixing Levi with a cold stare, Levi realized something else.

They weren't just questioning him.

They were investigating him.

Levi shifted against the hospital pillows. The IV in his arm tugged slightly, a reminder that his body was still recovering, but that didn't seem to matter to Burke and Hughes.

"Let's start from the beginning," Burke said, as he looked Levi directly in the eyes. His tone was even, calm, almost rehearsed. "You and your friends went to Superior National Forest for a bucks weekend. That right?"

Levi nodded. "Yeah. Rob is..." He stopped, the words catching awkwardly in his mouth. "Was getting married."

The correction felt like a punch to the gut.

"We wanted to do something different. No bars, no Vegas, just the five of us camping."

Burke scribbled something down. "Who was with you?"

"Rob, Carter and the twins Tyler and Tyson." Slowly, he read each name, each causing a sharp pang in his heart.

Burke flipped through his notes. "You've all known each other a long time?"

Levi nodded. "Rob and I grew up together. I met Carter in college, and the twins in high school. We've been close for years."

Burke nodded. "And you arrived... when?"

"Friday around noon, I'd say. We parked at a trailhead near Devil's Track Lake and hiked about four or five miles before setting up camp."

Hughes, who had been silent until now, spoke up. "Who chose the campsite?"

"Rob did," Levi said, glancing at his mom. "He used to go

there with his dad growing up.”

“Had you ever been there before?” Hughes asked.

“No,” Levi replied. “This was my first time, same as the others.”

Hughes jotted something down, then looked back up. “How was everyone's mood?”

Levi exhaled softly. “Everyone was excited. We were looking forward to spending a few days camping and fishing.”

Hughes tapped his pen against the notepad, thinking. “Did you take any weapons with you?”

Levi shook his head. “No.”

“No?” Hughes raised a brow. “Why not? There are bears out there. Wolves, maybe even mountain lions. Surely you've hunted before?”

“I have,” Levi said, then hesitated before adding, “but Tyler hated guns. When he was a kid, he saw his uncle get killed right in front of him. Ever since then, he couldn't stand them. So, whenever he was around, we didn't bring any. It was out of respect. We all knew how he felt about it.”

He glanced down briefly, then back up. “Besides, there

were five of us. Bears are usually afraid of humans. Five grown men would've been enough to scare one off. It just didn't seem like a big deal at the time."

Hughes paused for a moment before continuing. "What was the first night like?"

Levi's fingers clenched the blanket in his lap. "Quiet. Just a few weird sounds in the woods, but nothing that freaked us out. We laughed it off."

Burke made a note. "And the next day?"

"We went fishing. Spent most of the day on the lake. It was a fun day." Levi exhaled. "Until that night."

Burke glanced up. "What happened?"

Levi swallowed hard. "Rob found out Carter was having an affair with his fiancée."

Burke's pen stopped moving as he raised a brow.

"They got into it," Levi continued. "Yelling, shoving. I had to pull Rob off him. Carter stormed off, said he needed to clear his head. Went for a walk."

Burke leaned forward slightly. "Did he say anything as he left?"

Levi shook his head. "No, but we assumed he'd cool off and come back. He didn't."

Burke scribbled something down, his expression unreadable as he replayed Levi's response in his head. "What did you do?"

"We waited at first, but after an hour, we got worried. We grabbed our flashlights and went looking for him." A cold prickle crawled up Levi's spine. "We found him hanging in a tree."

Burke's expression didn't change. "Hanging?"

"Not like suicide," Levi said quickly. "Impaled. His body was skewered on a thick branch about fifteen feet up." His voice dropped. "Like something placed or threw him there."

His mother gasped softly from the corner.

Burke kept writing. "And you're saying something did throw him?"

Levi nodded. "Yes. How else would he get up there?"

Burke's pen scratched against the paper. "And that's when you knew something was wrong."

Levi swallowed hard. "Yeah. Very wrong. We ran back to camp. And that's when it really started."

Burke lifted his gaze. "What did?"

Levi hesitated, then forced the words out. "They toyed with us. Threw rocks, screamed, stayed just beyond the tree line. We could hear them moving."

Burke tilted his head. "Them?"

"There were three, at least." Levi's voice was quieter now. "Sasquatch. They were big. Bigger than any person, any animal. Covered in hair, but not just beasts. They were smart. They hunted us, one by one. They stayed hidden for the most part, but we did see their silhouettes, that night."

Burke and Hughes exchanged a look. Levi continued.

"Tyler was hit first," Levi said. "We didn't want to, but we had to gather firewood when something threw a rock the size of a football. It hit him in the side of the face."

Burke raised an eyebrow. "And then?"

"We carried him back to camp. He was out cold, but breathing." Levi drew a deep breath. "Then they distracted us. We heard movement behind the tent. When we turned, they had grabbed Tyler and were dragging him into the woods."

His breath came quicker.

"We wanted to go after him, but he was gone," Levi continued. "Tyson lost it. We barely held him back from running in after them."

"What happened next?" Burke asked as he glanced at Hughes.

Levi exhaled and glanced toward the window, his expression distant. "I think we tried to sleep, but they came into camp." His voice was quieter now, the memory clawing its way back. "As soon as it was light, the three of us decided to hike back to the trailhead and get help."

Burke nodded. "So, you left camp?"

Levi's fingers dug into the blanket. "We didn't make it far. Not long after we got on the trail, we came across this big tree blocking the path. It hadn't just fallen—looked like it'd been yanked out and laid there on purpose." He shook his head slightly. "It was too big to climb over. We had to go around."

His eyes grew distant for a moment.

"Before we moved, one of them walked out of the brush and grabbed Tyson." His voice wavered. "It broke his neck. Just like that."

Burke shot Levi a look from under his brow. "And you didn't run?"

"I did," Levi said. "So did Rob. We backtracked to a break in the trees and climbed down a rocky cliff. I figured if we stayed off the main trail, we'd have a better chance." He rubbed his palms against his thighs. "I thought we were paralleling it, keeping close without being out in the open."

He went quiet for a moment, his voice lighter when he spoke again. "We ran for most of the day. Then they caught up."

Burke's pen hovered over the paper. "Who caught up?"

Levi's throat felt like sandpaper. "One of the Sasquatch. It grabbed Rob, after he tripped." He exhaled shakily. "It dragged him off, screaming."

Burke's focussed eyes stayed on Levi. "But not you."

Levi's stomach churned. "I wanted to help him, but the damn thing was too fast. Rob disappeared within seconds. I kept running. I found a hollow log and hid inside it overnight."

Burke made a note. "Then what?"

"In the morning, I started moving again. I waded through a swamp, thinking maybe the smell would cover me. I thought I was heading for the trailhead, but I guess not." Levi gazed at the blanket. "They were still there. They let me think I had a chance. They waited until I was exhausted before they moved in."

Burke didn't react, just kept writing.

Levi looked between them. "That's when the helicopter saw me. If they hadn't been there…" He let the words trail off.

Burke paused before asking, "Were any of you drinking at camp?"

Levi hesitated.

"All of them were," he admitted. "Except me. I preferred to be the one with a clear head."

Burke nodded slightly, then adjusted his grip on the notebook. "How many guns do you have access to, Levi?"

"Three," Levi replied.

Burke glanced over his shoulder. "And you, sir?" he asked, directing the question to Levi's father.

"Four," his father said.

Burke scribbled a quick note. "Are they all registered?"

"Yes," they both answered at once.

Burke studied Levi for a moment before closing his

notebook.

"Alright, Levi. A search team has gone into the forest to look for your friends."

Levi's breath caught. "What?"

Burke studied his reaction. "They left this morning. They're combing the area where you were found."

A deep unease spread through Levi's chest as he sat up straighter. "They need to get out of there. Now."

Burke raised an eyebrow. "Why's that?"

Levi's pulse pounded. "Because those things will kill them too."

Burke sighed. "They're heavily armed, Levi. I think they'll be fine. Besides, the DNR posted two rangers at each trailhead in case any overenthusiastic Bigfoot hunters decide to go looking for him and his furry friends."

Levi couldn't imagine anyone willingly stepping into that forest after what he had endured.

Burke gave a final nod and stood. "Alright then. You all take care."

Hughes pushed off the doorframe with a quiet grunt.

"And Levi…" He paused at the doorway. "Don't go anywhere."

With that, the two detectives turned and left stepping out into the busy hall.

CHAPTER 2

Levi's mother kept glancing at him in the rearview mirror, her expression tense. His father sat in the passenger seat, staring straight ahead, his thoughts unreadable. The silence in the car settled between them, stretching longer with each passing mile.

No one knew what to say.

Maybe they thought leaving him alone was what he needed, or they were afraid of what he'd say next.

Or perhaps it was because of what the detectives had told him before they left the hospital.

"Don't go anywhere, Levi."

It wasn't an official order. They hadn't cuffed him or taken his passport. But it was a warning.

He was still a suspect.

They hadn't said it outright, but Levi could see it in Burke's face. They weren't sure if he was a victim or something else.

Levi stared out the window, realizing he was still living in a nightmare.

White Bear Lake looked the same as always. The water shimmered under the afternoon sun, rippling in the wind. The streets were familiar, the same stores, and neighborhoods he'd driven through for years.

Nothing had changed.

But he had.

They had driven past his house first, and the sight made his stomach lurch.

Reporters filled the front yard. Camera crews. Strangers holding signs. Some had candles, treating it like a vigil. Others held up their phones, waiting for him to appear, ready to record the moment like he was some spectacle.

One sign stood out.

"WHERE ARE YOUR FRIENDS, LEVI?"

His heart dropped.

His mother gasped. "Oh, Levi…"

His father mumbled something under his breath.

Levi stared at the sign, his stomach doing backflips.

Half of him wanted to throw open the door, rip the damn thing down, and scream at everyone to fuck off.

The other half just wanted to get the hell outta there.

Instead, he ducked down and wondered if his life would ever feel normal again.

"We're not stopping," his dad said.

Levi's mother drove on, through tears.

****

Levi's parents pulled into their driveway and parked. He stepped out, keeping his head low, not wanting to draw the attention of any neighbors.

Inside, the house was warm. The familiar scent of coffee hung in the air, with a faint trace of vanilla from an old candle. The hallway table still held framed photos of birthdays, family trips and younger versions of himself and his parents smiling back at him.

His mother set down her purse. "Go lie down, sweetheart. You need rest."

Levi didn't argue.

His bedroom still felt like his. The walls were a different color, and some things had been moved around, but it wasn't like he hadn't been here recently. The bed creaked as he sat down.

He should feel safe. But he didn't.

The second he closed his eyes, the memories surged forward.

Carter's body, impaled in the tree. Tyson's face before his neck was snapped. Rob's face twisted in fear before he disappeared into the brush.

Levi forced his eyes open.

****

A knock at the door.

His father stepped inside. He didn't sit on the bed or lean against the doorway. He went straight for the desk chair, lowering himself into it with a sigh.

Levi already knew what was coming.

"I need to ask you something," his dad said. "And I need you to be completely honest with me."

Levi braced himself. "What?"

His father hesitated, then met his gaze. "Did this really happen?"

It felt like the floor shifted beneath him.

Levi's breath caught. "What?"

His dad lifted a hand, like he was trying to keep him calm. "I'm not saying you made it up. But could there be another explanation? Shock, dehydration, exhaustion…"

Levi stood so fast the mattress groaned beneath him. "I know what I saw."

"Levi…"

"No." His voice came sharp, unsteady. "You think I imagined Carter's body impaled fifteen feet up? You think I just thought up Tyson's neck being snapped by an eight-foot monster? That I ignored Rob when he was screaming for me?"

His father exhaled through his nose, rubbing his temple. "I don't know what to think."

Levi scoffed. "That much is obvious."

His father didn't look at him for a long moment. Then he said, "I just want to understand."

"No," Levi snapped. "You don't. You just don't want to believe it."

His father finally met his gaze again, then gave a small nod. "Alright."

He stood and left the room.

Levi sat down on the bed, breathing hard.

He leaned forward, planting his elbows on his knees, his father's words echoing in his head. *Did this really happen?*

The doubt hit like a punch to the gut. His own father, the man who had raised him, taught him right from wrong, the man who was supposed to believe in him, thought he was either lying or had lost his mind.

And worse than that...

Did he think Levi had murdered his friends?

The thought twisted inside him, sick and disturbing.

Levi squeezed his eyes shut, but it didn't help. He could

still see his friend's last moments.

And his father thought he had done that?

A shaky breath left him.

He felt more alone now than he ever had in the forest.

****

Levi lay on his bed, staring at the ceiling, his thoughts tangled in everything that had happened when he heard a knock at the front door.

His mother's voice called up the stairs. "Levi? Abby's here."

For the first time all day, something in him eased.

He got up and headed down the stairs quickly.

Abby stood just inside the entryway, arms tucked into the sleeves of her sweater. Her dark hair was pulled back, and her brown eyes were soft, full of worry.

She gave him a small, hesitant smile. "Hey."

He didn't hesitate. He just stepped forward and pulled her into his arms.

She held on just as tight. "I'm so sorry."

His voice was quieter than he wanted it to be. "You believe me, right?"

She pulled back slightly, searching his face. "Of course I do."

Relief cut through the numbness. "Thank you."

But something in her expression shifted.

His stomach dropped. "What?"

She bit her lip. "I think you need space right now."

He took a step back. "Abby…"

She reached for him, but he didn't move. "Look, some of my coworkers know we're together. I work with patients every day, and if people find out I'm involved with you, it could cause problems for me." She hesitated, guilt flickering across her face. "I can't risk losing my job, Levi."

The words sat like a rock in his chest.

"So that's it?" His voice was steady, but there was something biting underneath.

"No. I just think you need time to deal with all of this. And I need to be careful, too. I wanted to come and see if you were ok."

He looked down at the floor. "Right."

Abby went to grab Levi's hand but stopped herself. "I'll call you soon, okay?"

Levi gave a single nod.

She hesitated, like she wanted to say more. Then she turned and left.

He stood there, staring at the closed door, wondering if that was the end of their relationship. Just like that.

A moment later, his mother's voice came from the hall. "Where did Abby go?"

Levi ran a hand through his hair. "Don't know. Don't care."

Claire frowned. "What happened?"

His tone was flat. "Being with me could result in her losing her job. Probably doesn't believe me either."

His mother stepped closer. "Levi, I believe you."

He let out a quiet scoff, shaking his head. "You believe me because you're my mom."

"That's not true," his mother replied.

His expression hardened, and he turned away, heading upstairs, taking the steps two at a time.

Levi laid on his bed, staring at the ceiling.

His father didn't believe him.

His best friends were dead.

And now, Abby was slipping away too.

They all thought he was crazy.

And maybe they were right.

Because as much as he tried to shake the feeling, it wouldn't go away.

His life was changed forever in every way.

CHAPTER 3

SUPERIOR NATIONAL FOREST

The ridge was quiet. Wind shifted through the high grass and low pines, carrying the smell of sweat, fear and something burned.

Aluk stood motionless, tall and broad as a tree trunk, staring down at the winding trail below. His hair stirred faintly in the breeze, dark against the pale sky. Beside him, Matto crouched low on thick limbs, one hand in the dirt, the other curled tight against his chest. Tahkan stayed further back, resting on his haunches, eyes wide and alert.

Ten of them. Hairless ones.

They were close to where the first bodies had been taken. Not close enough to smell the blood anymore, but close enough to feel the tension in the air. The hairless ones knew they were being watched, even if they couldn't see from where.

Matto shifted his weight and made a low chuffing sound, questioning and sharp. His gaze didn't leave the humans.

Aluk gave no reply at first. He just watched. Then, slowly, a low grunt rolled from deep within him. Firm. Final.

"No."

Matto turned toward him, head tilted. Another short grunt. A gesture, barely more than a twitch of fingers toward the trail. He wanted to go after them now. End it before the thunder sticks were used.

Tahkan made a sound low in his throat. He was the youngest. Still learning when to speak and when not to. He looked from Matto to Aluk, waiting for the answer.

Aluk didn't move. His voice was steady when he rumbled again.

"No. Not now. They are looking for the ones we ended."

His arms remained still at his sides, but the meaning carried clear in the tone and the weight of the sound. Patience. Strategy. Not fear, but calculation.

"They have thunder sticks. They see well in the light. They will come back soon, in the dark. That is when we end them with the help of the clan."

Matto lowered his head slightly. Not quite a bow. Not quite agreement. But he said nothing else. He understood what Aluk meant.

Tahkan rose slightly, eyes scanning the trees beyond the trail.

With a series of grunts, *"They will keep looking. "For the one we brought to the sanctuary."*

Aluk nodded once. A small, slow movement.

"They will come."

The wind shifted again, rustling the pine needles and lifting dust from the ridge. The three stood in silence, watching as the humans disappeared briefly around a bend in the trail, then reemerged. They were spread out now, the last hairless one glancing behind every few steps.

Tahkan crouched again, keeping still. His hands rested in the dirt, fingers twitching faintly.

The hairless ones paused at a clearing and gathered in a loose circle. One of them knelt, pointing at something on the ground. Tracks. Maybe blood.

Aluk watched with grim satisfaction, knowing they would never find the bodies.

CHAPTER 4

Levi stood outside his bedroom, barefoot, the hallway floor cool beneath his feet.

He hadn't meant to stop. He was heading to the kitchen for water, trying to ignore the anxiety that had taken root in his chest since he came home. But as he passed the closed door to his parents' room, he heard his name.

And then his mother's voice, harsher than usual, raised just above a whisper.

"Why don't you believe him?"

There was a pause. Then his father's voice, lower and strained, like he was forcing calm.

"It's not about belief, Claire. It's about logic. Think about what he said. A bunch of Bigfoot killed his friends!" Cole let out a long, slow breath. "It sounds absolutely ridiculous."

Levi didn't mean to listen. But he didn't move either. His body stayed frozen just outside their door, heart thudding against his ribs.

Claire's voice came again, tired but insistent. "He came home covered in blood and scratches. Clearly traumatised, Cole. And not once has he changed a detail. Not once. You really think he made this up and killed his friends?"

"No," Cole said. "No, I don't think he killed anyone. God, Claire, I can't even begin to imagine that. He's our son. He wouldn't do that. Especially not to his friends. But this story..."

His voice faltered for a moment. Levi closed his eyes.

"I just can't wrap my head around it," Cole said. "I want to. I've tried. But every time I sit down and think it through, it sounds like something out of a nightmare. A delusion. It doesn't make sense."

There was silence behind the door for a few seconds. Claire's voice dropped low.

"You think he's lying?"

"No." Cole answered immediately. "I think he believes it. I just don't know if it really happened the way he says."

The sound of fabric shifting followed, like someone turning away.

Then Cole spoke again.

"Have you even turned your phone on lately? You haven't, have you?"

More silence.

"I have," Cole said. "And it hasn't stopped. Calls. Voicemails. Strangers calling Levi a murderer. People saying we're hiding something. Someone from Bumfuck, Iowa left a one-star review on my business page, saying I raised a killer and should be locked up."

Claire sobbed quietly.

"And it's not just that one," Cole went on. "There are dozens now. Full paragraphs. Accusations. One of them said they hope I lose everything. That no one should support a company run by the father of a mass murderer."

Levi's stomach turned.

Cole's voice cracked slightly. "How do we carry on with this over our heads, Claire? How does Levi? We don't know when the detectives are coming back or what they believe. This could destroy everything. My business. Our name. Us."

Claire didn't answer right away. When she finally did, she spoke through tears.

"So you don't want to support him?"

"Of course I do." Cole's voice rose, pained. "But we have to be honest about what this is. The world doesn't care what we believe. It only sees the headline. 'Five men enter the woods. One comes back.' That's all they need."

Claire said something too soft for Levi to make out.

Cole answered with a sigh. "I don't know what to do anymore."

Levi stepped back, careful not to let the floor creak. His chest hurt. He turned away from the door and walked silently back to his room, shutting the door behind him.

He sat on his bed, staring at the floor, hands clenched in his lap.

He didn't blame his father. Not really. If someone had told him the same story just a month ago, he wouldn't have believed it either. But hearing those words out loud, knowing the doubt was real, not just in strangers' voices online, made it worse.

It wasn't just the story people couldn't believe. It was him.

CHAPTER 5

Levi stared down at his soup, absently pushing a piece of carrot around with his spoon. The rich scent of homemade broth and fresh bread filled the air, but he barely tasted any of it. His appetite had been gone since he left the hospital, but his mother had insisted.

"Something warm," she had said. "Something good for the soul."

Claire had made everything from scratch. Chicken noodle soup with thick egg noodles, fresh parsley and tender shredded chicken. Warm, buttered bread straight from the oven. She had even set the table properly, like it was a holiday dinner.

But it wasn't.

It was an attempt at normal.

But normal was gone.

Cole sat at the head of the table, eating slowly, barely making a sound. His brows were pulled together in deep thought, his mind somewhere else entirely.

Levi's mother took small sips, eyes flicking between them both, searching for something to say.

She gave up.

No one talked.

The clock above the fridge ticked softly, the sound filling the dead space in the room.

Levi took another slow sip, but the soup tasted like nothing.

He wasn't sure how long they sat there like that. A few minutes. Maybe longer.

Then, a loud knock at the front door.

Everyone's head turned.

Levi's pulse picked up. His father wiped his mouth with a napkin and pushed his chair back.

"I'll get it," Cole said, standing up.

The knock came again. Louder.

Claire silently hoped it wasn't the media or the detectives. Levi stayed in his seat, watching as his father made his way to the door.

Cole barely had it open before voices came through, clear, demanding, frantic.

"Where is he?"

"Where's Levi?"

Cole stepped outside onto the porch, blocking the doorway. Levi already knew who it was before he heard their names.

Isaiah and Monica Reed.

Tyler and Tyson's parents.

Levi's stomach twisted.

His mother's chair scraped against the floor as she stood up.

"Levi..." she started, but she didn't finish.

He was already moving.

****

The cold evening air hit Levi as he stepped onto the porch.

The Reed's stood at the bottom of the steps, their faces full of grief and confusion.

Monica's eyes landed on him first, and whatever self-control she had left shattered.

"Boy, you better tell me what happened to my babies," she said, voice trembling. "You better not stand there and lie to my face!"

Isaiah's eyes were building with grief and suspicion. His hands were fists at his sides, his entire body rigid with anger and devastation. He took a slow step forward.

"Where are they, Levi?" His voice was quieter, but it carried just as much force. "Where the hell are my sons?"

Levi choked up. "I..."

Monica cut him off. "You listen to me. You look at me, in my damn face, and you tell me the truth!" Her voice cracked, her chest rising and falling with every breath. "Don't you lie, Levi! Not to me!"

Levi's heart pounded but he met her gaze.

"I'm not lying," he managed.

Isaiah's nostrils flared. "Then why don't none of this make sense?"

Levi forced himself to hold their gaze, but the guilt was crushing. They weren't here to accuse him of killing their sons. They just wanted answers. They wanted something that would let them sleep at night.

But Levi had nothing to give.

His voice was hoarse when he spoke. "I told the police everything."

"That ain't good enough!" Monica's voice broke, and she let out a choked sob, pressing a hand against her mouth.

Isaiah reached for her arm, steadying her, his own face twisted with grief. "You better hope they find my boys."

Levi took a deep breath.

He felt the words rise up before he could stop them. "I don't know why I made it." His voice was tight, almost unsteady. "I haven't a clue why I'm the one who came back, and I am so sorry that Tyler and Tyson didn't."

Monica stared at him, her expression crumbling.

Isaiah's jaw tightened. "We need to know," he said. "Did they suffer? Did they run? Were they scared?" His voice dropped lower, more ragged. "Did they call for us?"

Levi's stomach churned.

Yes.

They did.

They were terrified.

But how the hell could he say that?

How could he look them in the eyes and tell them their sons died in terror, knowing they would never get their bodies back?

Levi opened his mouth, forcing the words out.

"They didn't suffer. It was quick."

It wasn't true, not entirely. But it was the only mercy he had to offer.

Monica let out a wail, her knees buckling. Isaiah caught her, wrapping his arms around her as she sobbed against his chest.

Cole took a step forward. "I am sorry, but I think you should go."

Isaiah looked at Levi one last time, shaking his head.

"If you ain't told the whole truth yet, you better pray it don't come out later." His voice was low. "'Cause if I find out you been lying…" He didn't finish. He didn't have to.

Cole moved, stepping between them. "I think that's enough."

Isaiah swallowed hard, pulling Monica closer. He nodded once, then turned and walked back toward their car, his wife still crying in his arms.

Levi stood there, frozen, until the taillights disappeared down the street.

His father stared at Levi. "Inside."

****

Levi sat on the couch, staring at nothing.

The house was silent again, but it wasn't the same as before. The quiet had changed. It felt worse now.

His mother sat beside him, rubbing his arm in slow circles. "Levi, honey…"

He didn't respond.

She sighed, pressing a kiss to the top of his head before standing up and retreating to the kitchen.

Cole lingered near the door, rubbing his jaw. He seemed like he wanted to say something, but in the end, he just shook his head and walked upstairs.

Levi sat there as Isaiah's words played over in his head.

Did they suffer?

He closed his eyes.

Yes.

Yes, they did.

And now, their parents would never be able to bury their children.

CHAPTER 6

ROB – SASQUATCH SANCTUARY

The first thing Rob felt when he drifted back to consciousness was the ache. A bone-deep exhaustion that made him question if he was even awake at all. The thick vines wrapped around his stomach dug into his ribs, pinning him against the rough bark of the tree. He could shift slightly, enough to relieve some of the pressure, but not much else.

His arms were free, but that hardly mattered when he had nowhere to go.

His hands bore the raw marks of his first few days here. He had still believed escape was an option then. He had clawed at the vines, yanked at them until his skin was rubbed raw and bloody.

That was days ago. Maybe longer.

Time had become a blur, a loop of drifting in and out of consciousness. Hunger gnawed at his stomach. His throat was raw from thirst. He had tried to count the days, but the endless cycle of waking and passing out made time feel meaningless.

On the second night he was there, a low rustling in the brush nearby made his pulse quicken. He turned his head slowly, not wanting to draw attention, and saw a young Sasquatch.

He was crouched just outside the tree line, half-hidden behind a cluster of ferns. His hair had a copperish tinge that caught the fading light. He was smaller than the others, probably a young juvenile.

He had come before. Watching. Curious.

This time, he brought something.

A handful of small berries. And a plastic water bottle.

Rob's eye's widened at the sight of the bottle. It was unmistakably human. A crumpled Dasani, its label peeling, dented like it had been kicked around before being found.

The Sasquatch must have scavenged it from somewhere.

Rob swallowed hard, his tongue felt like sandpaper. He

didn't know where the berries came from, but right now, he didn't care.

The young one grunted softly, a sound that wasn't quite a growl but carried a questioning tone. Then he backed away, disappearing into the brush.

Rob hesitated only a second before reaching down, stretching against the tight band of vines around his waist. His fingers wrapped around the bottle first, the plastic crinkling as he lifted it.

The water was warm and slightly stale, but he didn't care. He tilted it back, gulping greedily, water dribbling down his chin as he drank too fast. The relief was instant.

The young Sasquatch—Rob had started calling him *the copper one* in his head—was the only one that acknowledged him.

The rest barely spared him a glance.

The females walked past without looking in his direction, their eyes fixed on their work, their movements efficient and controlled. The young ones never ventured too close, as if they had been told not to trust him.

The males ignored him entirely, except when he moved too much. If he shifted too suddenly or leaned forward too far, they would growl or hiss a warning that needed no translation.

Rob learned quickly to stay still.

They didn't want him dead—at least, not yet.

But they didn't want him here either.

****

Rob shifted as much as his restraints allowed, rubbing a sore spot on his ribs where the vines pressed too tightly. He had nothing to do but watch.

And so he did.

The Sasquatch weren't just a group of wild creatures.

They were a community. Despite being nine-foot monsters that had brutally killed his friends, there was something unsettlingly fascinating about them.

During the day, the females moved through the forest, gathering berries, roots and plants. They carried what they found in woven satchels made of thick grass and bark. Some used crude wooden tools to dig through the soil, searching for tubers.

They always worked in pairs or groups, never alone. The

young ones, small and lanky with thick, shaggy hair, stayed close to the females, playing and tumbling through the brush. They climbed trees with ease, their movements almost ape-like but more controlled. When the females returned to the cave, the young followed closely, mimicking them and learning.

The males spent most of the day watching or sleeping. Some stayed near the treeline, standing motionless for hours. Others moved quietly through the brush, always alert and always patrolling. But at night, they vanished. Rob had watched them leave just after sunset, slipping into the darkness without a sound.

The first night, he had thought they were abandoning him. Then they returned. Dragging carcasses with them.

They always ate inside the cave. Rob never saw them consume anything, but the smell of blood and raw meat carried through the air.

It wasn't just hunting. It was organized. They weren't just animals. They were something else.

****

One night, the cold was unbearable.

His body shuddered violently, muscles locking up in

spasms. His teeth clattered together so hard he thought they might break.

The night stretched on forever.

His thoughts drifted in and out of focus, his head heavy from exhaustion and dehydration. He dreamed while he was awake, images flashing through his mind that didn't make sense. He saw Levi's face. His mother's kitchen. The warm glow of a fireplace he could almost feel against his skin.

Then another image. A cave.

Not this one, but something familiar. Firelight dancing against rock. Figures moving in the glow. A deep, distant thrumming in his ears, like something ancient whispering just beyond his understanding.

He blinked, his vision swimming.

The cave was gone.

Only the dark remained.

He barely registered the sound of rustling brush when the copper-haired one appeared again, crouched in the same spot as before.

This time, he didn't bring food.

He dropped something different onto the ground. A bundle of bright-colored fabric.

Rob reached for it with stiff, cold fingers.

A flash of bright orange.

His stomach clenched.

Tyson's windbreaker.

He lifted it with trembling hands, his heart sinking.

The last time he saw it, Tyson was wearing it when the Sasquatch snapped his neck on the trail.

Rob's heart dropped.

Had it been ripped from Tyson's body?

Why had the Sasquatch kept it?

The young one made a low, uncertain grunt, shifting his weight.

Rob's entire body locked up, his chest rising and falling too fast.

Tyson was gone.

Slowly, he pulled the windbreaker over his arms. The

fabric was stiff, torn, but it was better than nothing.

His hands clenched the sleeves as he let out a slow, shaky breath.

He appreciated the copper-haired one's kindness.

Even if it came at the cost of a memory he wasn't ready to face.

****

One night, after the hunting party returned, the mood in the clearing shifted.

The largest of the males, the one who had taken him, stepped into the open, a fresh kill slung over his back. A huge buck. Its legs dangled limply, its body streaked with dark blood. With a grunt, the Sasquatch hoisted the carcass off his shoulder and let it drop onto the ground with a heavy thud. The smell of iron swept through the air.

The Elder approached. His posture was steady, his expression unreadable. He stopped just short of the kill and let out a low, rumbling grunt.

Rob didn't understand the words, but he didn't have to.

The hunter straightened, his broad frame tense, breath coming harder through his nose. His fingers curled into tight fists before he made a sharp gesture toward the trees, his voice rough, a string of short, clipped chatter followed by a growl.

The Elder remained still. He didn't interrupt, didn't react. He only watched. Then, after a long pause, he gave a single grunt.

And then, he looked at Rob.

A shiver slid over Rob's body.

The hunter exhaled harshly, then bent and lifted the deer again, hoisting it back onto his shoulder like it weighed nothing. Without another sound, he turned and walked toward the cave. The others followed, slipping into the darkness behind him.

Rob let out a slow, shaky breath.

He didn't know what had just happened.

But he knew one thing.

The one who had taken him wasn't happy.

And that was dangerous.

CHAPTER 7

The next morning, Levi made the mistake of turning on the new phone his mother had given him.

They'd started fresh with a new number—no voicemails, no texts, nothing carried over from before. That had been the point. A clean slate.

But instead of leaving it alone, Levi opened the browser, typed in his name, and made an even bigger mistake.

His name was everywhere.

"WHITE BEAR LAKE SURVIVOR OF FOREST TRAGEDY UNDER SUSPICION."

"ONLY ONE MAN CAME OUT—WHERE ARE THE OTHERS?"

"DOES LEVI HOLLOWAY KNOW MORE THAN HE'S SAYING?"

"MAN CLAIMS BIGFOOT KILLED HIS FRIENDS, BUT LET HIM

GO."

Every article, every segment, every social media post. It was all the same. People weren't just doubting him. They were calling him a killer.

"This guy straight-up murdered his friends and came up with the dumbest cover story in history."

"Sasquatch? Really? Why not aliens? Why not a damn wendigo? How stupid does he think we are?"

"Mark my words, Levi Holloway will be in handcuffs by the end of the month."

He scrolled through comment sections, barely blinking.

Murderer. Liar. Psychopath.

The worst part wasn't the anger. It was the certainty.

They didn't think he might be lying. They knew it.

A few people defended him.

"Y'all are so sure he's lying, but what if he's not? People go missing in the woods all the time."

"My uncle saw something like this when he was hunting in '96. He still won't talk about it."

But those voices were drowned out by the rest.

The overwhelming consensus was simple.

Levi Holloway was a liar. Levi Holloway was a killer.

The only question was why.

****

Levi stared at the phone in his hands.

His pulse thudded in his ears, too fast, too loud.

What the hell was he supposed to do?

What could he do?

Even if he went to the police, begged them to look harder, it wouldn't matter.

Because they weren't listening.

Because no one believed him.

****

A soft knock at the door.

His mother's voice. "Levi?"

He closed his eyes for a second, then forced himself to answer. "Yeah."

The door cracked open. Claire stepped inside, her expression gentle but cautious. Like she was approaching a wounded animal.

She held her phone in her hands. "Detective Burke called me."

Levi's stomach clenched. He set his own phone down, bracing himself. "And?"

She hesitated. "The search party... they didn't find anything."

The words barely registered. "What?"

Claire sat on the edge of the bed, fingers laced together. "They checked the area you gave them. They searched for hours yesterday. They found your campsite."

Levi sat up straighter. "Good."

She didn't nod.

"They said it was mostly intact. Like no one ever left."

His mouth went dry. "No."

"They didn't find bodies, Levi." She said it softly, like she was afraid of what it would do to him. "No blood. No sign that anyone else was ever there."

He shook his head. "That's not possible."

She swallowed hard. "The detectives don't know what to do with this."

Levi barked out a laugh. It sounded wrong. "They know exactly what to do. They're gonna say I made it all up."

"Levi."

"No, Mom, he said as he stood. Look online. Look at the damn news." He threw a hand toward his phone. "Everybody already thinks I'm guilty. Now there are no bodies? No evidence? Are you kidding me?"

His mother stood too, reaching for his arm. "Levi, please, just…"

He pulled back before she could touch him. Not because he was angry at her.

Because he was terrified.

Because he had seen what happened.

Because they were dead.

Because their bodies should be there.

But they weren't.

And now, no one would ever believe him again.

Levi sat back down on the bed, running both hands through his hair.

His mother stood beside him, helpless.

He stared at the floor, voice hollow. "They're covering it up."

Claire blinked. "Who?"

"The DNR guys." He looked up at her. "The ones in the helicopter. The ones who pulled me out of there."

Her brows pinched together. "Levi, what are you saying?"

"They saw them." He clenched his fists. "They saw the things chasing me. I know they did."

She didn't argue.

Because she already knew what he was going to say next.

"They won't talk," he said. "If they go public, they lose everything. Their jobs. Their reputations. Who's gonna listen to some backwoods government biologist claiming he saw a Sasquatch?"

His mother sat beside him again, smoothing her hands

over her lap.

She didn't tell him he was wrong.

Because she knew he wasn't.

****

A sudden knock at the front door.

Claire startled. Levi sat up straighter.

They both turned toward the hallway, listening.

Three more knocks. Loud. Forceful. Urgent.

Levi shot his mother a look.

She was already standing. "Stay here."

Levi got up anyway. "Mom."

"Levi." Her voice left no room for argument. "Stay here."

She turned and disappeared down the hall.

Levi took a slow breath, listening as she made her way to the door.

Then, silence.

Whoever was out there wasn't saying anything.

His mother's voice came, soft but steady. "Can I help you?"

Nothing.

Then, a voice.

A man's voice.

"Mrs. Holloway, we need to speak with your son."

Levi's stomach twisted.

He took a step toward the hallway.

His mother spoke again. "Who are you?"

CHAPTER 8

R igid and staring, Levi sat on the couch, his gaze fixed on the men before him.

They didn't look like law enforcement.

No badges. No suits. No polite, rehearsed questions.

These men looked like they belonged in a war zone, not his mother's living room.

The one in charge sat directly across from him.

Tall. Broad-shouldered. Cold, piercing eyes that didn't blink more than necessary. His face giving nothing away. Every movement was deliberate, efficient, like a man who never wasted energy on things that didn't matter.

His name was Jonah Briggs, and from the second he walked through the door, your eyes naturally followed him.

Claire sat stiffly in the chair beside him, her hands

pressed into her lap. She hadn't said a word since they arrived, but Levi could feel the tension in her posture. She was trying to hold it together, but he could tell she wasn't sure if she could trust them.

Jonah clasped his hands together, elbows resting on his knees. His presence was controlled, but something about him felt coiled, waiting.

"We need to talk," Jonah said.

Levi didn't blink. "Yeah? What about?"

Jonah didn't hesitate. "Your trip to Superior National Forest."

Levi sighed, shaking his head. "If you're here to tell me I'm full of shit, get in line."

Jonah's expression didn't change. "I'm not."

That stopped Levi cold.

Jonah sat back slightly, gesturing to the men beside him. "This is Echo Black. We operate off the books. Special operations. That's all you need to know."

Levi glanced at the other men and women. Their expressions were unreadable, but he could feel their eyes assessing him, waiting to see how he'd react.

His stomach twisted. "Why are you here?"

Jonah leaned forward. "Because I believe you. We believe you."

His mother gasped.

Levi's pulse ticked up. He had spent the last few days being torn apart by the media. Mocked. Accused. Branded a liar and a murderer. Now this man, this stranger, was sitting in his house telling him that he believed him?

Levi narrowed his eyes. "Bullshit."

Jonah didn't react.

"The Superior National Forest is home to a few clans of Sasquatch," he said. "Not nomads. A population that have been there since before you or I were born."

Levi's stomach twisted. "And you know this how?"

Jonah held his gaze. "Because it's our job to know."

Levi sat back.

Jonah studied him for a beat, then said, "Your story isn't unique. People disappear in those woods all the time."

A chill crept up Levi's spine.

Jonah continued. "In fact, two other men went missing around the same time as your friends. Their truck was left at the trailhead. No sign of them since."

Levi's breath stalled.

He sat up, leaning back on the sofa. "Why the hell haven't I heard about that?"

Jonah's expression didn't change. "Because no one's looking for them. No family pushing the media, no cops asking questions. They were just your average nobodies."

Levi exhaled slowly, nausea curling in his gut.

Jonah's tone never changed. "They're escalating. What happened to your group wasn't just an attack. It was a statement."

Levi rubbed his hands over his face. "What do you want from me?"

Jonah didn't waste time. "Do you think any of your friends are still alive?"

Levi's heart did a somersault.

"No," he said flatly.

Jonah's eyes stayed on him. "You're sure?"

Levi's shoulders sagged with the breath he released. "I saw them die. I heard their bones break. I heard them scream." His voice wavered slightly, but he pushed through. "Carter. Tyler. Tyson. They're gone."

Jonah didn't move. "And Rob?"

Levi hesitated. His skin felt too hot, like something was clawing at the inside of his ribs.

"I saw him get dragged off," he admitted. "One of them took him. Pulled him into the trees." He sighed. "But they killed everyone else. Why the hell would they keep him alive?"

Jonah glanced at one of his men, then back at Levi.

"They don't always kill," he said. "Sometimes, they take."

Levi's pulse hammered.

His mother gasped, covering her mouth with a hand.

Jonah leaned forward, his eyes serious. "We've seen this before. Humans go missing, but not all of them die. Some are held. Some are used."

Levi's stomach twisted. "Used for what?"

Jonah didn't answer.

Instead, he let the silence settle.

"We need to find him," Jonah continued. "You narrow down the area on a map, we do recon and go in."

Levi stared at him. His thoughts felt slow, heavy, tangled.

Finally, he forced himself to speak. "Why?"

Jonah met his eyes. "What?"

"Why would you go in there to see if he's still alive?" Levi's voice was quiet but firm.

Jonah's answer was just as steady. "It's our job."

Levi shook his head. "The Sasquatch will kill you before you even find where they live."

Jonah didn't blink. "We're highly trained. We've done missions like this many times before."

Levi didn't know what to say to that.

These men and women were soldiers, professionals, something else entirely. But him? His mother? They weren't sure if they should trust them.

Levi exhaled, glancing toward his mother. She was anxious and wide-eyed.

Slowly, he nodded. "Give me a map."

One of the men pulled a folded topographic map from his pack and spread it across the coffee table. Levi stared at it, pulse thrumming in his ears.

His hand hovered over the paper, fingers trembling slightly.

Levi hesitated for only a moment before pressing his finger against the map.

"That's where the camp was, and this is where the Sasquatch were hiding all damn night, taunting us, screaming and throwing rocks."

Jonah studied the spot before dragging his finger across the map. He tapped a location farther away. "And this is where you ended up when the helicopter picked you up."

Levi frowned, leaning in. His stomach twisted when he saw the distance.

He had known he ran. He just hadn't realized how far.

He wrinkled his brow. "Jesus… I was miles off the trail."

Jonah didn't respond. He studied the map for a moment, then looked back at Levi. "How many did you see?"

Levi swallowed. "Three. One was huge. Another was big but not as big. The third looked younger, smaller. Maybe a juvenile, I don't know."

Jonah nodded slightly. "Anything else that would help us?"

Levi shook his head. "No." He looked Jonah dead in the eye. "But *if* Rob *is* alive, you get him out asap."

Jonah held his gaze. "That's the plan."

Levi exhaled, sinking into the couch. He dragged a hand down his face, his mind spinning.

Jonah stood, adjusting the strap on his vest. "We'll be in touch."

Without another word, the rest of the team turned and walked out, silent and efficient. No goodbyes, no reassurances. Just ghosts disappearing into the daylight.

Levi sat there, staring at the door. He wanted to believe Rob was still alive, he needed to.

But after everything he'd seen, hope felt more like a lie he kept telling himself.

CHAPTER 9

Claire watched Levi pace the living room as she sat on the couch.

"I don't know who those men really work for," Claire said, her voice careful. "But maybe… maybe this is a good thing. If Rob is still alive, hopefully, they can find him."

Levi scoffed. "Mom, you don't get it."

She frowned. "What don't I get?"

He stopped pacing and turned to her, frustration flickering behind his exhaustion. "How big they are," he said, his voice rough.

Claire's forehead creased. "Levi…"

He pointed up, his hand shaking slightly. "Look at the ceiling."

She glanced up, hesitant.

"These are ten-foot ceilings, right?" Levi asked.

She nodded. "Yeah."

His eyebrows tightened. "Because they're *that* tall." His voice dropped, firm and certain. "At least four feet wide. And that's just the ones I saw." He shook his head. "The biggest one? You can't possibly fathom its size."

Claire's face was unreadable, but he could tell she was trying to process it.

Levi paced, his mind racing. "And the worst part? They move *faster* than anything that size should. They're at home in the forest, completely in control. They have every upper hand. You don't hear them until they want you to. You don't see them until it's too late. They are not just animals. They are far more intelligent than you can imagine."

Something in Claire's face shifted.

She had believed him before, but now she felt it.

Her mouth parted slightly, but no words came out.

Then her face crumpled.

Tears welled up in her eyes before spilling down her cheeks.

Levi's stomach dropped.

"Mom?" His voice softened, concern replacing his frustration.

She shook her head, shoulders trembling.

"Mom, what's wrong?"

Claire wiped at her tears, but they kept coming. Her voice wavered. "I believed you, Levi. I believed everything you told me." She let out a shaky breath. "But seeing the fear in your eyes just now…" Her chest rose and fell in uneven breaths. "It gave me a glimpse of what you went through."

Levi sighed. He felt clammy, but he pushed past it and put his hand on her shoulder.

Exhaling deeply, he replied. "I hope to God Rob is alive, and I hope they bring him back." His voice dropped slightly. "But I'm not getting my hopes up until I see him. I can't."

His mother let out a soft, broken breath, then stood and pulled him into a hug.

A tight, desperate embrace.

For a second, Levi just stood there, tense. Then his shoulders dropped, and he let himself sink into it.

His mother held him like she was afraid to let go.

And for the first time in days, Levi let himself grieve.

CHAPTER 10

Levi wasn't sure how his mother convinced him to go. Maybe it was the exhaustion, maybe it was the way she had said it, soft but firm. "Let's get out of the house for a little while. Your favorite place. My treat."

He had barely eaten since getting home. Everything tasted like ash, like nothing. But he nodded anyway.

A few minutes later, they were in the car, heading for town. His mother didn't fill the silence with questions or attempts at comfort. She let him be.

The town felt smaller than it had before. Or maybe Levi just felt different inside it. The streets were the same, the stoplights still flickered red and green, and the gas station on the corner still had the same half-broken sign that no one ever fixed. But Levi wasn't the same.

They pulled into the small burger joint he had loved since he was a kid. A local spot, the kind with greasy paper bags and fries that tasted better than anything else in the world.

Claire ordered for him. She didn't need to ask what he wanted.

They ate in the car. His mother talked about nothing important, filling the space with small, easy things. Levi let the warmth of the food settle in his stomach, let himself pretend just for a few minutes that things were normal.

But the feeling didn't last.

The closer they got to his parent's home, the more the anxiety crept back in.

And then they saw her.

A figure sat on their porch steps, her arms wrapped around herself.

Levi recognized her immediately.

Bree.

His gut clenched, but his face stayed blank.

He stepped out of the car, as if he didn't notice her. Claire hesitated, her eyes flicking from Bree to Levi.

"I'll be inside," she said carefully.

Bree stood as Levi approached. "Hey."

Levi didn't respond. He walked right past her, taking the porch steps two at a time.

"Levi, please. I just want to talk."

He stopped at the door, exhaling heavily before turning. His expression was unreadable, his voice flat. "I have nothing to say to you."

Bree looked shocked. "Why?"

Levi let out a quiet laugh, but there was no humor in it. He shook his head and finally met her eyes. "Because the last thing my best friend was thinking before he was taken was that his fiancée was sleeping with his friend."

Bree's mouth parted slightly, her face going pale. "Levi…"

"Yeah." His tone was cold. "We all found out that first night. Carter confessed."

She flinched at the name, her hands clasping together. "I…"

"Don't."

He shook his head in disgust.

Bree swallowed. "I never meant…"

Levi didn't care.

He turned, opened the door, and walked inside.

The door slammed shut behind him.

CHAPTER 11

ECHO BLACK

The Echo Black convoy rumbled along the gravel road leading to the Devil's Track Lake trailhead in the Superior National Forest. Just before the entrance, a park ranger stepped out of his SUV, parked at an angle across the road. He adjusted his belt and approached as the two matte black Chevrolet Suburbans came to a stop.

Jonah rolled down his window and held up his ID. The ranger gave it a quick glance, nodded, and stepped aside, waving them through without a word.

The air was cool but comfortable, hovering in the mid-50s. A steady breeze drifted through the trees as a Pileated Woodpecker hammered against a nearby pine. The sun had burned off most of the morning mist, but the forest remained dense with shadows.

Jonah stepped out first, scanning the area for anything that didn't belong. The midday light caught the sharp angles of his face, his features framed by a thick beard and a goatee streaked with specs of silver. His piercing blue eyes swept the tree line with the quiet patience of a predator. Broad-shouldered, built like a warrior from another era, he moved with the controlled grace of a man who had spent his life hunting dangerous things.

Whisper emerged next, silent as his name. He was leaner, with wiry muscle and a stillness that made him unnerving to watch. His dark hair was cropped short, his eyes always moving, calculating. The others joked he never blinked. Dressed in a matte black tactical jacket, Whisper opened the back of one Suburban, retrieving his drone cases before setting them on the ground. The latches clicked as he flipped them open, revealing four sleek, high-tech drones resting in custom slots.

Bringing up satellite feed now," Rook said from the open door of the second SUV, his fingers moving over his tablet. His screen filled with a high-altitude thermal scan of the forest, courtesy of a private military satellite.

Jonah leaned against the SUV, watching the screen over Rook's shoulder. "Time delay?"

"Five minutes," Rook confirmed. "Won't help with real-time movement, but if something's been through recently, we'll catch it."

Jonah gave a small nod. "Do it."

Rook worked fast, overlaying the most recent scan on top of previous images. The forest stretched out in crisp infrared, cold and undisturbed.

Whisper powered up the first drone. The small aircraft hummed softly as its rotors spun to life. One by one, the others followed, their dark matte bodies reflecting almost no light.

"Launching primary recon," Whisper announced.

Jonah watched as the drones lifted into the sky, silent and smooth. Their cameras fed live data to each team member's tablet, displaying thermal, LIDAR, and high-definition optical feeds.

"Expanding search radius to ten miles," Whisper said. "Starting with the coordinates Levi gave, then pushing outward."

Jonah checked his watch before getting back in the SUV. The recon had begun.

CHAPTER 12

Echo Black wasn't just a special operations team, they were the kind of unit whispered about in the corners of briefing rooms, deployed when the job called for ghosts instead of soldiers. Each member had been pulled from different corners of the world, brought together not by rank or medals, but by one simple fact: they got results.

Jonah "Ghost" Briggs is the commander, and the oldest on the team. Ex-Delta Force, calm under pressure and cold when he needs to be. Years in the field stripped him of illusions. He leads with clarity, makes decisions without hesitation, and earns loyalty not through speeches, but by always walking out front. If you're going to war, you want Ghost on your side. He's a man of few words, but when he speaks, everyone listens.

Samira "Valkyrie" Kasim is second in command. Born to a Turkish-American family and raised in a household that demanded strength, she served as a combat medic in SOCOM before moving into black operations. Hazel-eyed and highly intelligent, she combines precision with grit. She never blinks at pressure, she just narrows her eyes and keeps moving.

Darius "Havoc" Jefferson is the muscle. A towering brute with a grin that means trouble and a build like a freight train, he comes from Force Recon and has a reputation for getting up close and personal. When others back off, Havoc steps forward. If a door needs breaking, he doesn't look for hinges.

Logan "Diesel" Cartrell is the firepower specialist. Once a demolitions expert in Afghanistan, he went dark and never looked back. Quiet, methodical, and fluent in the language of fire and steel, he carries a flamethrower like most carry a rifle. Nobody ever asks him twice about his past. The team respects the silence.

Jack "Breaker" Williamson is chaos wrapped in sarcasm. Former Aussie SAS, sharp-eyed with a sharp tongue to match. He brings the explosives and the dark humor, always the first to volunteer when the odds are worst. If there's a trap to be set or a wall to be breached, Breaker is already reaching for the detonator.

Xavier "Rook" Davis, the youngest on the team, handles logistics, surveillance and tech, but when things get kinetic, he holds his own. Smart and fast, he started with a keyboard in an NSA bunker and ended up on the battlefield. He's got something to prove, and Echo Black gave him the chance.

John "Whisper" Kowalski is the quiet eye in the sky. Drone pilot, recon expert, and all-seeing ghost. Nobody really knows where he came from, some say CIA, others say private sector. He never confirmed either way. Whisper sees what others miss, tracks what others lose, and no one knows drone tech better than he does.

Miguel "Reaper" Cortez is the sniper. Cold, efficient, and unreadable. He never misses. He worked for JSOC once, maybe something darker before that. He treats stillness like a weapon. No one ever sees him flinch, not even in the middle of hell.

Riley "Wildcat" Morgan is speed, precision and edge. Raised in the underbelly of a city that forgot its name, she cut her teeth in gang wars before rising to elite contract work. She's lethal in close-quarters and moves like smoke through alleys or steel hallways, and when her blades come out, she doesn't miss.

When the threat comes, Echo Black answers.

CHAPTER 13

ECHO BLACK

The first hour of recon passed with nothing but the odd deer or two grazing.

The drones swept over dense trees, rocky outcroppings and narrow game trails. The satellite images remained unchanged, showing nothing but untouched wilderness.

The second hour crept by, the team cycling through every imaging mode possible. Thermal scans revealed nothing but scattered deer, black bear, and one wolf pack. LIDAR imaging mapped the terrain, but dense rock formations made visibility difficult. SAR (Synthetic Aperture Radar) detected no unnatural structures or movement.

Split between two SUVs, the team stayed connected through their comms.

Breaker let out a slow breath over the channel. "Feels like we're chasing ghosts."

Wildcat smirked from the passenger seat. "Maybe we are."

Jonah ignored the chatter. His eyes stayed on his screen, scanning the endless trees.

"We're missing something," he said.

At 2:17 p.m., Rook sat up straighter in the second vehicle. "Wait."

Jonah's voice came through the comms from the first SUV. "What is it?"

Rook's fingers flew across his tablet, overlaying two satellite images side by side. One was from twenty minutes ago. The other was the most recent update.

"There's a shift here," Rook said, enlarging an area of the forest near a rocky incline.

Jonah leaned toward his monitor. At first, he didn't see it. Then, he noticed the subtle difference.

A small section of the canopy had shifted, barely noticeable, but enough.

"That's not wind," Reaper said, his tone flat. "Something moved through there."

Jonah narrowed his eyes. "Whisper, focus the drones on that location."

"On it," came the reply.

The drones adjusted course, flying low over the rocky incline where the satellite anomaly had been detected.

For thirty minutes, they swept the area. Nothing.

Then, Whisper's voice cut through the radio. "I've got something."

Jonah sat forward. "What?"

"Thermal scan picked up a brief heat signature. Big. Then it vanished."

Jonah frowned. "Run it back."

Whisper replayed the footage in slow motion.

The thermal camera briefly flickered, detecting two massive heat sources, then nothing.

Jonah frowned. "Where'd they go?"

Reaper studied the screen. "They must have moved

under dense cover. A thick tree, maybe a rocky overhang."

Jonah exhaled slowly, his mind working through the possibilities. The disappearance of the heat signature didn't mean they were gone, it just meant they knew how to blend into their environment.

Whisper adjusted the drone's trajectory, directing one toward a narrow trail leading away from the rocky enclave.

It led directly to a lake.

Valkyrie spoke first. "That's got to be their water source."

Jonah watched as the drone camera panned out, revealing the lake's full size. The screen displayed the name in the corner. Devil's Track Lake.

Rook read it aloud, then frowned. "Hell of a name."

Breaker smirked. "Bet the locals didn't call it that for nothing."

Havoc scratched his chin. "Think the name came from them? The tribes knew something lived here?"

For a moment, no one answered.

Then Wildcat leaned back. "You ever notice how many places have names like that? Devil's Peak. Ape Canyon.

Booger Hollow. Feels like every state's got a dozen spots with 'Devil' or 'Ape' in the name."

Breaker chuckled. "Yeah, and none of them got those names 'cause some settler saw a cute little deer prancing through."

Reaper nodded. "Happens all over. The natives call something a bad place, settlers ignore it, then people start disappearing."

Valkyrie scoffed. "And yet no one listens."

Havoc folded his arms. "So what do you think? Locals here saw something and called it Devil's Track because they saw some big ass footprints?"

Wildcat smirked. "Booger Hollow's my favorite."

Breaker grinned. "Yeah, imagine the first guy who said, 'Hey, let's settle down in Booger Hollow.'

Jonah didn't say anything.

He kept his eyes on the drone feed, watching as the camera followed the narrow trail winding toward the lake.

CHAPTER 14

ECHO BLACK

The matte black Chevrolet Suburbans idled at the trailhead, their engines humming softly against the quiet of the forest. The air held a crisp bite, the kind that settled into your lungs and lingered.

Jonah stood near the open rear hatch, watching as Whisper worked his tablet, recalling the drones. The primary recon units adjusted course, veering back toward them, while one remained behind, hovering in the dense tree cover near the rocky enclave.

"That last one's staying?" Rook called out, watching the feed on his own screen.

Whisper nodded, his fingers moving with precise efficiency. "Passive recon mode. Won't move unless it detects activity."

Jonah studied the screen. The remaining drone had already settled into a stationary position, partially obscured by branches, recording everything within its field of view.

Before calling them back, the drones had captured two distinct heat signatures—something large, something that could only be Sasquatch. They had confirmation now. The terrain recon would continue back at the cabin, but the hunt had officially begun.

"If anything changes," Whisper added, "we'll know."

Jonah gave a slight nod. "Pack it up."

The team moved quickly. The retrieved drones were secured, their gear loaded back into the vehicles. Within minutes, the convoy pulled away from the trailhead, rolling south toward Pincushion Mountain.

****

The dirt road was rough, full of dips and loose gravel that made for a bumpy ride. The Suburbans handled it well, their reinforced suspensions absorbing most of the impact, but it was slow-going. The drive would take about twenty-five minutes.

Havoc gripped the wheel, his large hands steady despite the uneven terrain. At 6'4", he was a wall of muscle, built for carrying heavy firepower and kicking in doors. A scar ran along his jaw, half-hidden by a neatly trimmed beard, a souvenir from a mission gone sideways years ago. His voice was a deep rumble as he flicked his gaze between the treeline and the road ahead. "Feels weird driving away after finding something like that."

Jonah didn't look at him. "We weren't learning anything else from the trailhead."

In the back, Whisper barely moved, his fingers gliding over his tablet. "Stealth drone is transmitting. No movement yet." His voice was quiet, detached, as if reading from a script.

Reaper sat beside him, arms crossed. "That cave is a goddamn stronghold. They've got sentinels, access to water, and deep cover. I bet they've been there a long ass time."

"No need to move. They've got everything they need," Jonah said.

The second Suburban followed close behind. Inside, Rook scrolled through satellite images, flipping between different filters.

"That cave network is bigger than I thought," he said into the radio. "Gonna need to analyze the scans once we get back."

****

The rented cabin sat at the end of a narrow, tree-lined driveway, tucked far enough from the main road that no one would casually stumble onto it. A large wooden structure built for seasonal use, it had enough space for ten, with an open living area that now served as their command center.

The second the team stepped inside, the air shifted. The drive had been quiet, but here, surrounded by their gear and screens filled with real-time intel, they switched back into mission mode.

Whisper set up his drone station near the fireplace. Rook and Breaker took the dining table, their screens already displaying LIDAR scans and satellite comparisons. Valkyrie and Wildcat leaned against the wall, listening as Jonah pulled up a chair.

Havoc, meanwhile, dug into his vest pocket and pulled out a protein bar.

"Jesus, man," Wildcat said, watching as he ripped the wrapper open with his teeth. "I swear, if you don't have one of those every two hours, you start looking like you might tear someone's arms off."

Havoc took a slow, controlled bite, chewing as he met her gaze. "Gotta feed the machine."

Breaker smirked. "One of these days, we're gonna be in a firefight, and he's gonna be reloading with one hand and eating with the other."

"Yeah," Rook added, "and I bet the bullets will be dipped in peanut butter for extra protein."

Havoc flipped them both off without missing a bite.

Jonah didn't even acknowledge the exchange. He had already settled into his chair. "Talk to me."

Breaker scratched at the scruff along his jaw, leaning forward slightly. He was shorter than some of the others but built like a brick wall, all corded muscle, and reckless energy. His brown eyes had a playfulness to them, always glinting with amusement like he knew a joke no one else did. His Australian accent gave every word a cocky, laid-back edge, the kind that made it sound like he wasn't afraid of much, and that anything he was afraid of, he'd probably charge at head-on anyway.

Rook tapped his tablet, throwing an image onto the monitor. It was a high-resolution satellite shot of the rocky enclave near Devil's Track Lake. He flipped to a second image, taken an hour later.

"Something moved," he said.

At first glance, the two images looked identical. But when Rook zoomed in, a section of small tree cover near the rock formations had shifted.

Reaper leaned in, his gaze narrowing. "No way that's natural."

"Definitely not," Rook said. "The canopy's been pushed aside. Something big moved through here."

Jonah studied the screen. "Whisper?"

Whisper was already pulling up LIDAR scans. "The cave system is bigger than we thought. Temperature fluctuations suggest deep tunnels. The heat signatures we picked up were close to the entrance."

Breaker let out a low whistle. "That's a lot of room for things to bloody hide."

Jonah exhaled through his nose. "Then we're going to confirm how many we're dealing with."

He turned to Whisper. "Send the drone in. Start with the perimeter."

The screen switched to a new feed as a small, silent drone detached from one of the larger ones. The camera view jerked slightly as it maneuvered through the underbrush, moving low and slow toward the rocky enclave.

No one spoke.

The drone's night-vision engaged as it weaved between the trees. The thermal scan flickered, multiple large heat signatures appearing.

For the first time, they saw them as they were.

A monstrous figure sat hunched on a rock, arms resting on its knees. Another walked among the trees, moving slowly. Further back, near the entrance, a third crouched low, picking at something on the ground.

They weren't hiding.

They were living.

"Jesus," Valkyrie said.

Reaper couldn't take his eyes off the screen. "This is their home."

The drone hovered, shifting its angle. As it adjusted, the camera caught something new.

A man.

Tied to a tree.

The team went completely still.

The drone hovered closer, its camera stabilizing. His mid-section was bound with what looked like vines. His head hung forward, dark hair matted against his forehead. His chest barely moved, but he was breathing.

Rob.

Jonah's voice was quiet. "Hold it there."

Whisper adjusted the drone's position, angling the camera slightly. It lingered on Rob for another few seconds, long enough to confirm he wasn't dead.

Then the drone continued toward the cave.

The entrance was barely visible, a jagged opening partially obscured by thick brush and shadows. The thermal scan flickered, picking up residual heat inside, but nothing clear enough to identify.

Then something moved.

A gigantic hand gripped the edge of the rock wall. Thick fingers. Long thick nails. A deep exhale sent a cloud of mist into the air.

Then the sentinel turned its head.

Not toward the cave. Toward them.

The drone's feed flickered. Static crawled across the screen.

The last thing they saw was a gigantic hand reaching toward the camera.

The screen cut to black.

Silence filled the cabin.

Breaker let out a slow whistle. "Damn, he was an ugly bugger."

Wildcat exhaled. "Most of them are."

Jonah stared at the blank screen for a long moment before speaking. His voice was calm, but there was an edge to it.

"We've confirmed where they are and that Rob is still alive," he said. "Next is to analyze the terrain and how we get in."

CHAPTER 15

ECHO BLACK

The smell of spiced beef and slow-simmered beans filled the cabin, cutting through the crisp mountain air drifting in from the cracked windows. The team gathered around the wooden dining table, plates in front of them, screens glowing in the background with maps, drone footage and satellite overlays.

Havoc stood at the stove, stirring a large pot of chili with the kind of focus most men reserved for disarming explosives. The scent of roasted peppers and slow-cooked meat thickened the air, a reminder that they hadn't eaten since that morning. He grunted as he tasted a spoonful, nodding in approval.

"You're lucky I'm cooking," he said, tapping his spoon against the rim of the pot. "If it was Breaker, we'd be eating

MREs."

Breaker smirked from where he sat at the table, stretching out his legs. "Oi! I make a mean spaghetti. And by 'make,' I mean 'boil noodles and dump in a jar of sauce.'"

Wildcat snorted. "So you don't make spaghetti. You make regrets."

Reaper, leaning against the counter, didn't look up from his screen. "Can we focus?" His voice was quiet, but there was a hint of impatience. "We're on the clock."

Jonah sat at the head of the table, elbows resting on the wood, his eyes locked on the monitor where Whisper had pulled up the latest drone footage. Rob was still tied to the tree, slumped against the trunk, unmoving except for the slow rise and fall of his chest. The vines around his waist looked tight, his head hanging forward.

"How long has he been in that position?" Jonah asked.

Whisper barely stirred, his fingers effortlessly gliding over his tablet. "Nearly four hours. No movement except slight head shifts."

Reaper didn't look away from the screen. "They haven't fed him."

Valkyrie frowned. "That we've seen."

She leaned forward slightly, her hazel eyes focussed as she studied the footage. Her dark hair was pulled back into a tight, practical braid, the strands barely shifting as she moved. Her olive-toned skin, a mark of her Turkish heritage, contrasted against the dim cabin lighting. Years of operating in the most dangerous parts of the world had shaped her into someone who rarely wasted words, her quick wit matched only by her precision on the battlefield.

"They haven't moved him either," Rook said, eyes scanning the footage. "If they were planning to take him inside the cave, wouldn't they have done it already?"

Wildcat shook her head. "Or they're waiting for something."

Jonah exhaled slowly. "Either way, we don't wait for them to decide."

The team ate quickly, the sound of spoons scraping against bowls filling the air between conversations. Despite the warm food, no one looked relaxed. They weren't just eating; they were fueling up before the real work began.

Whisper rewound the drone feed, this time focusing on the movement around the cave. The Sasquatch weren't lurking or pacing. They were living.

Valkyrie leaned forward, watching. "They don't look worried."

Reaper kept his eyes on the screen. "They don't have to be."

Jonah scanned the footage, expression unreadable. "Sentinels?"

Whisper switched feeds. The camera zoomed in on two figures, one standing at the top of the rocky cliff above the cave, the other positioned further down, partially obscured along the narrow trail leading to the sanctuary. Both were perfectly still, their hulking forms blending into the darkness.

"They rotate in shifts," Whisper said. "Four-hour intervals, maybe three. No gaps. One set leaves, another takes over."

Jonah's jaw tightened slightly. "Then we have no window."

Breaker set his bowl down with a dull thud. "That's not great for us."

"No," Jonah agreed. "It's not."

Valkyrie drummed her fingers against the table. "We kill

one, another takes its place. No openings, no weak spots."

"So we create one," Wildcat said.

The table fell silent.

Breaker leaned forward. "Sniper fire." His voice calm. "Take the sentinels out before they can alert the others."

Jonah's gaze flicked to Reaper. "You make that shot?"

Reaper didn't hesitate. "I make that shot."

Jonah exhaled through his nose, nodding. "Then we go tonight."

Silence fell on the room for a moment, everyone processing what had just been set in motion. There was no turning back now. They all knew what this meant, once they moved, there would be no second chances.

Rook cleared his throat, breaking the silence. "That leaves one issue. Getting him out."

Jonah didn't need to ask what he meant. The lake.

"A boat," Valkyrie mumbled.

Jonah leaned back slightly. "Where are we getting one?"

Rook was already typing. "There's a small marina about

nine miles from here. Mostly personal-use speedboats. We need something fast but quiet."

Diesel, who had been mostly silent until now, shook his head. "Nothing's gonna be fast and quiet."

Jonah nodded. "We'll take speed over silence once we're clear of the shoreline."

Rook scanned through listings. "We could steal one."

Breaker smirked. "Borrow."

Rook rolled his eyes. "Fine. Borrow. But we'd need to grab it soon. It'll take at least an hour to haul it to the lake, plus another ten minutes to launch."

Wildcat set her bowl down, tilting her head slightly. "How long from the lake to Rob's position?"

Whisper adjusted his screen, switching to a topographic map showing Devil's Track Lake in relation to the rocky sanctuary. The path was narrow and uneven, with thick undergrowth. A relatively small ravine cut through part of the terrain, likely formed by an old creek bed. It wasn't deep, maybe twenty feet down give or take, but it would slow them down, forcing them to find a way across.

"No vehicle access to the lake," Whisper said. "The old

service road's been cordoned off with a metal gate."

Breaker glanced up. "Gate like that won't hold. One good hit or a set of bolt cutters and we're through."

"Roughly half a mile on foot from the shoreline," Whisper continued. "Twenty-minute approach time, factoring for terrain."

Jonah considered that. "Total time from here to the cave?"

Rook typed quickly. "Twenty-five minutes to the marina, an hour to hook the boat and get it to the lake, another ten to get it launched. Then a twenty-minute hike to Rob. About two hours, give or take."

Havoc scooped another bite of chili. "So when do we leave?"

Jonah checked his watch. "We roll out at 22:00 hours."

Reaper, still watching the drone footage, finally spoke. "That means we'll reach Rob's position between 00:30 and 01:00."

Wildcat exhaled. "Hopefully that means a bunch of them are out hunting."

The room went quiet as that sank in. If she was right,

they'd have fewer bodies to deal with. If she was wrong, they'd be walking into the middle of a full clan.

The team finished their meal in silence, knowing the next time they sat down together, things could be very different.

Jonah stood. "Let's go get the boat."

CHAPTER 16

SASQUATCH SANCTUARY

The males were restless. Since nightfall, they had been shifting in place, their breathing deep, muscles coiled with energy. The hunt should have begun already, instincts pulling them toward the trees, toward the chase.

But they had not left.

Because the Elder had not given the order.

Instead, he sat unmoving at the center of the cave, firelight flickering across his broad shoulders.

Aluk.

Matto.

Tahkan.

They stood before him now, waiting.

At the entrance, the sentinels remained still, waiting for the Elder's command.

And yet, something unspoken hung between them all, a decision the Elder had not yet voiced, but one that had already taken root.

He raised his hand.

A deep grunt rumbled from his chest, commanding their attention.

Aluk did not move.

Matto stood tense, shoulders squared.

Tahkan shifted slightly but did not speak.

The Elder inhaled, then exhaled slowly through his nose.

The clan waited.

Then, his hands moved.

A low, rolling snarl vibrated in the Elder's chest, followed by a short, harsh bark. His hands moved in slow, deliberate gestures.

"You wanted war." The elder stated.

A flicker of images followed, sent outward for all to see.

A hairless one running.

A hairless one left alive, captured instead of killed.

The rest of his kind returning for him.

The Elder's nostrils flared, and he let out a slow, rumbling huff.

Then, another sharp grunt, a demand.

"Why? The elder asked.

The Sasquatch shifted. A low, uneasy chatter spread among them.

One of the males near the entrance emitted a deep growl, his disapproval clear.

Another followed.

Matto stepped slightly away from Aluk.

Tahkan lowered his gaze.

Aluk remained still.

But not silent.

A slow chuff left Aluk's throat, deep and steady, his posture firm. Then, his fingers moved, slashing through the air in fast, controlled motions.

"The hairless ones would have come eventually." Aluk responded.

A rumble of deep, clicking chatter rippled through his chest.

Then, another pulse of imagery followed.

Humans swarming the land like ants.

Red-breath spreading through the trees, devouring everything. Thunder sticks raised. The clan forced to fight.

Aluk's upper lip pulled back, his chest expanding as he sent one final message, reinforced with a feral growls.

"They come. Always. So we bring them now to end them." Aluk said.

A test.

A reckoning.

A war.

He did not deny the Elder's accusation.

He embraced it.

For the first time, the Elder's breathing deepened, his shoulders rising slightly. A slow, deep rumble, akin to a growl, escaped him as he shifted, letting Aluk's words sink in.

Then, the Sasquatch responded.

A sharp, rolling bark echoed from the clan, a challenge from one of the males.

Another.

A third.

Matto's massive hands curled at his sides, his throat vibrating with a low chuff of unease.

Tahkan remained still, silent.

The Elder inhaled deeply, his chest expanding, before releasing a slow, rolling huff.

Then, he lowered his palm toward the earth, a sign of finality.

A deep, rumbling chatter followed, his hands shifting in firm, controlled movements.

"The hairless one will not stay." The elder said.

An intense, resonant grunt followed.

"After the hunt." The elder added.

The Sasquatch stirred immediately, letting out low, eager clicks and chuffs.

The tension had shifted.

The hunt had been delayed long enough.

When they returned, the hairless one would be dealt with.

Aluk did not bow his head.

He said nothing.

And then, finally, the hunt began.

****

ROB

Rob shifted slightly, pulling Tyson's windbreaker tighter around his shoulders. The bitter cold bit through the thin fabric, but it was better than nothing.

He didn't know what time it was.

Didn't know how long it had been since the sun had set.

He just knew the nights were getting colder.

He sat with his back against the tree, his arms wrapped around himself as much as the vines would allow. His breath curled around him, faint mist against the darkness.

His mind drifted.

To Levi. To Carter. To the twins. He could still hear their voices sometimes, buried in the back of his mind—laughing, arguing, making plans for a future they'd never get to have. He thought of their families, of the grief they must be drowning in, waiting for news that would never come.

Then his parents. His mother's voice, soft and full of warmth. His father's steady presence. They would be wondering if he was dead in these woods, if he had suffered, if there was anything left to bury. The thought twisted something deep in his gut.

And then there was Bree.

The moment he thought of her, a biting pain speared through his chest. Not from his injuries. Not from the cold. Something worse.

She had betrayed him.

The last time he saw her, she had smiled at him like she

always did. Kissed him. Told him she loved him. And all the while, she had been with Carter.

His stomach churned. It didn't matter now. None of it did. Carter was dead. The others were dead. And soon, he might be too.

****

The forest had changed.

The Sasquatch were moving.

Rob had started to learn their patterns, which ones left, which ones stayed behind.

But something about tonight felt different.

The air was heavier. The sentinel at the treeline and on the cliff stood more rigidly, their gazes sharper.

Rob swallowed hard.

Maybe it was just his mind playing tricks on him.

Or maybe it wasn't.

Maybe tonight was different.

He had no way of knowing that his fate had just been sealed.

CHAPTER 17

ECHO BLACK

The marina sat in near silence, the dark expanse of Lake Superior stretching endlessly beyond the docks. A few scattered boats rocked in the water, their hulls reflecting the dim glow of overhead lights.

Jonah Briggs stepped out of the SUV first, scanning the lot.

"Keep it quiet," he said, already moving toward the docks.

Behind him, Breaker, Valkyrie and Diesel followed, dressed in dark, non-reflective gear that helped them blend into the shadows. Whisper and Rook had stayed back at the cabin, monitoring the mission remotely. They had pinpointed the location of a 25-foot Scarab speedboat, exactly what they needed for a fast extraction.

****

Rook sat in front of three screens, tracking their movements in real-time. He tapped his tablet, adjusting the satellite feed.

"You're clear so far. No movement in the lot," he said.

Whisper, seated across from him, barely looked up from his own monitor. "Security cameras are looped. You've got a window, but don't take your time."

Rook flicked through another feed. "One guard on-site," he added. "Older guy, he's in the south lot right now. Just keep your heads up."

"Copy," Jonah said, his voice low and motioned forward. "Let's move."

****

The lot held several trailers, all parked in neat rows near the boat ramp. Some were locked, but others weren't. Whisper had scouted ahead using satellite imaging, marking a few possibilities.

Diesel strode toward one of them, crouching near the hitch. He gave it a once-over, then nodded. "This'll do."

Breaker raised a brow. "What if the owner comes back

looking for it?"

Diesel didn't answer right away. He just reached into his vest, pulled out a hammer, and broke the lock with a hearty thump. "We'll bring it back," he said flatly.

Diesel was incredibly fit, standing at 6'1", built like a linebacker with broad shoulders and thick arms. His dark hair was kept short, and his expression rarely changed from calm, calculating, and unreadable.

Valkyrie smirked. "It's not stealing. It's government-sanctioned borrowing."

Breaker sighed. "If we keep 'borrowing' stuff, we're gonna owe the government a hell of a lot of interest."

Diesel ignored them, hooking the trailer up to the Chevrolet Suburban. Once it was secured, he climbed into the driver's seat and started backing it into position near the ramp.

Jonah gave a short nod. "Let's move."

****

They spread out, keeping to the shadows. The marina was mostly deserted at this hour, but there was always a risk, cameras, late-night fishermen, and, of course, security.

They reached the boat dock without incident. The Scarab sat in its slip, sleek and fast, with a deep-V hull built for cutting through waves. A powerful Mercury Racing engine sat at the stern, a beast built for speed.

Breaker let out a low whistle. "Now that's a damn fine getaway ride."

Valkyrie pulled a set of lock picks from her vest and crouched beside the gate leading to the docks. "Give me thirty seconds."

She slid the picks into the lock, her fingers moving with precision.

Jonah scanned the lot again. Still clear.

The lock clicked open.

Valkyrie smirked. "Ladies first?"

Breaker stepped past her. "After you, princess."

They moved down the dock swiftly. Diesel unhooked the mooring lines while Breaker climbed into the boat and started working on the ignition.

Valkyrie glanced at the empty slips around them and shook her head. "We're lucky it's not a few weeks later," she said. "By mid-November, most of these boats would be gone before the lake starts freezing near shore."

Breaker snorted. "Yeah. Good thing for us this rich asshole hadn't put his toy away yet."

Diesel grunted. "Means we don't have to steal from some old guy who spent his retirement fixing up his dream boat. I can live with that."

Jonah ignored the conversation, his senses sharpening. Something wasn't right.

The hairs on the back of his neck stood up.

Footsteps.

Slow. Steady.

Then a voice.

"Can I help you?"

All four of them went still.

A security guard stood at the end of the dock, a flashlight resting on his belt, hand near his radio. He was older, mid-sixties, with the build of someone who had worked security long enough to know when something wasn't adding up.

Jonah turned first, his expression unreadable. He

stepped forward smoothly, his gloved hand reaching into his vest.

The security guard's eyes tracked the movement.

Jonah pulled out a badge.

It gleamed under the dim dock lights, a simple government issue with a laminated card.

The security guard frowned. "That's…"

Jonah said nothing.

The guard's gaze flicked to the badge, then back to Jonah's cold stare. Then back to the badge.

A long pause.

The others remained tense, waiting.

Finally, he exhaled through his nose, rubbed his jaw, then turned and walked away without a word.

Breaker let out a breath. "Well, that was easy."

Valkyrie smirked. "Guess the badge worked."

Diesel snorted. "Worked because of who was holding it. No one wants to question a guy with that face."

Jonah ignored them, turning back toward the boat. "We're on the clock. Move."

****

Breaker pushed a screwdriver forcefully into the ignition, twisting to get it to turn over. The engine roared to life, smooth and clean.

Valkyrie untied the last line and climbed aboard. Breaker took the wheel, steering the Scarab out of the slip.

Jonah and Diesel stayed on the dock until the boat was fully out, then turned and walked back toward the truck.

By the time the Scarab reached the ramp, Breaker was already wading in, guiding it onto the trailer.

The second his boots hit the water, he sucked in a quick breath. "Jesus Christ, that's cold!" He shook his head. "I think my balls just turned into ice cubes."

Valkyrie chuckled. "That's assuming you had any to begin with."

Breaker shot her a glare but kept working, teeth clenched against the chill.

Valkyrie cut the engine and climbed out, securing the winch line to the boat. Breaker cranked the winch, pulling the Scarab onto the trailer. Once it was in place, Diesel latched the safety chain.

"Smoothest boat heist I've ever pulled off," Valkyrie said.

Breaker wiped the lake water off his hands. "Yeah, because you've done so many."

Jonah didn't comment. He shifted into drive, pulling forward slowly as the Scarab settled on the trailer. Once it was secure, he gave a small nod. "Let's go."

They climbed back into the truck, pulling out of the marina lot.

Jonah took one last glance in the rearview mirror.

The security guard stood at the edge of the docks, watching them go.

Not calling it in.

Not stopping them.

Just watching.

Jonah said nothing. He just kept driving.

They had their boat. Now all that was left was the rescue.

CHAPTER 18

ECHO BLACK

Jonah backed the trailer down the dirt driveway, the Suburban's taillights glowing red in the dark as the cabin slowly emerged from the shadows. Pincushion Mountain loomed in the distance, its dark silhouette rising against the night sky.

He killed the engine and stepped out, glad to have that task taken care of. The others followed, boots scuffing against the packed dirt as they headed for the steps.

Breaker rolled his shoulders. "Well, that was a hell of a field trip."

"Yeah," Valkyrie said, slamming the truck door. "We borrowed a boat, and a trailer, and scared the shit out of a security guard. Productive night."

Diesel gave a grunt of approval, heading for the cabin's porch. "We haven't even got started yet."

They moved quickly, stepping into the warmth of the cabin. A stone fireplace sat cold and empty, the wooden floors creaked under their boots, and the heavy scent of coffee hung about from earlier.

Whisper was inside, sitting at the dining table with a laptop open, multiple windows of drone footage and satellite recon pulled up. Rook sat beside him, scrolling through something on a tablet, one boot propped up on the table like he owned the place.

"All good?" Whisper asked without looking up.

Jonah pulled off his gloves and tossed them onto the table. "Yeah. No issues."

"Besides Breaker almost freezing his balls off," Valkyrie added.

Rook smirked. "And here I thought he didn't have any to begin with."

Breaker threw his beanie at him, which Rook dodged without effort.

Diesel made a beeline for the fridge, yanking it open and

grabbing a bottle of water. "Alright, we got the ride. What's next?"

Jonah checked his watch. 21:15. They had forty-five minutes before final prep and departure.

Whisper glanced at his tablet, then looked at Jonah. "Found something that might make this a little easier when we get across the lake."

Jonah lifted a brow. "Go on."

"About 450 yards down from where we originally planned to offload, there's an old dock." Whisper tapped the screen, enlarging a grainy satellite image. "Did some digging. Used to be a campground there. Got shut down in 2010." He smirked slightly. "Easy to hazard a guess why."

Diesel leaned over to get a look. "Dock still holding up?"

Whisper nodded. "Looks solid enough. From what I saw on the drone, the planks aren't completely rotted out, and the support beams are intact. It'll be easier than trying to land on sand or gravel."

Jonah studied the image for a moment, then gave a short nod. "Good. We'll use it."

"Hydrate, gear up, and be ready to move," he said to the

room.

Most of the team grabbed drinks from the fridge, water, sports drinks and energy bars.

At the far side of the room, Havoc grabbed a pair of adjustable hand weights and started curling them, pumping up his arms as he spoke.

"Can't show up looking weak," he said, switching arms.

Breaker shook his head. "You really think a few curls are gonna help you win a wrestling match with a ten-foot Sasquatch?"

Havoc grinned. "Hell no, but if I'm going out, I wanna look good."

Valkyrie rolled her eyes. "You think they care if you're shredded?"

"They might," Havoc said, still lifting. "Maybe they respect strength."

"Or maybe they just rip off your head," Rook said.

Havoc snorted. "Guess we'll find out."

Jonah let the conversation flow around him as he unzipped his duffel, checking his weapons. SCAR-H, FNX-45

Tactical, Kukri knife. Clean, loaded, ready.

"How many do you think we're dealing with?" Jonah asked, glancing at Whisper.

Whisper didn't hesitate. "Easily more than a dozen, at least. Maybe twenty. Maybe more."

That made Breaker pause. "Biggest clan we've gone after in a while."

"Yeah," Wildcat said. "Most we've taken down in the past year was what, seven? Eight?"

Diesel nodded. "But those were smaller units. Nomadic ones. This is different."

"Because they're settled," Whisper said, tapping a few keys. "They have a structure, a home. They aren't just moving through."

Jonah gave a short nod. "And that makes them more dangerous."

The room fell silent for a moment. Not because they were afraid. Because they understood.

This mission wasn't just about taking down a threat.

It was about retrieving a human hostage from their

stronghold.

And that changed the game.

Havoc set down the weights and flexed his arms. "You know what I wanna know?"

Valkyrie sighed. "Oh, this should be good."

Havoc grinned. "What do you think Sasquatch meat tastes like?"

The room went quiet for a second.

Then Breaker groaned. "Jesus, man. What the hell?"

Diesel smirked. "You're assuming we'd live long enough to find out."

Havoc shrugged. "I'm just saying, we eat bear, elk, deer. Why not?"

Whisper finally looked up from his laptop, expression unreadable. "If you ever get the chance, you can take a bite out of one and let us know."

Rook chuckled. "Havoc's gonna be the first dude in history to get a Sasquatch burger."

Then, from the corner, Reaper spoke.

"Alright," Reaper said, leaning forward. "Let's settle it. What the hell are these things?"

Wildcat groaned, rubbing her temple. "Oh, not this again."

"We've been over this," Diesel added, rolling his eyes. "It doesn't matter."

"It matters," Reaper insisted. "You've seen how they move. You've seen how they disappear. And you definitely never heard of civvies finding bodies or remains."

Breaker exhaled. "So what? You think they're Nephilim?"

Reaper shrugged. "Maybe. Or something even older. Every ancient civilization has stories of giants. Maybe they didn't all die out."

"Or maybe they're something we aren't meant to understand," Whisper said.

Valkyrie shook her head. "Or maybe they're just really good at staying hidden. I don't blame them personally. Humans suck."

Diesel leaned back, arms crossed. "Or maybe the government already has them. You don't think they've got live ones locked up somewhere?"

Rook smirked. "Of course they do. They let us take 'em out in the field, but you bet your ass some are in labs somewhere. No way we're the only ones in the loop."

Havoc scoffed. "So what, they've got a Bigfoot farm somewhere? Raising 'em like livestock?"

Whisper tapped his laptop. "We know for a fact there are places like Dulce Base, deep underground. Who knows what's locked up in those labs?"

Reaper stayed quiet for a moment. "All I'm saying is, whatever they are, they aren't just animals."

Jonah, who had been silent, finally spoke.

"It doesn't matter what they are." His voice was calm, cold. "They bleed. They die."

That was the end of the conversation.

Jonah checked his watch again. 21:45. Fifteen minutes.

"Suit up," he said, grabbing his gear. "We move out at twenty-two hundred."

No more jokes.

No more downtime.

It was time to get serious.

One way or another, by sunrise, this mission would be over.

And not all of them might make it back.

CHAPTER 19

ECHO BLACK

The cabin was silent except for the sound of zippers, clicks and the soft rustle of gear being prepped. Echo Black didn't need words. They had done this enough times to know what came next.

Jonah stood at the center of the room, tightening the straps of his tactical vest. His SCAR-H, loaded with armor-piercing 7.62x51mm rounds, sat on the table beside his FNX-45 Tactical. The suppressor was already locked onto the rifle, reducing muzzle flash and noise while keeping its lethality intact.

Across from him, Havoc checked the belt feed on his Knight's Armament LAMG. The 7.62x51mm AP rounds in the belt would tear through bone and muscle like paper. His Glock 20, loaded with 10mm Auto armor-piercing rounds, sat in a secure drop-leg holster.

"Last call for gear," Jonah said. His voice was quiet but firm.

No one responded. They didn't need to.

Breaker adjusted the straps on his plate carrier, securing the weight of his SCAR-H with an M320 grenade launcher mounted beneath. Forty-millimeter high-explosive rounds were tucked into his pouches, ready to be deployed if things got bad. His Glock 20 rested at his hip, a dependable backup.

Rook crouched beside his gear, methodical as ever. He locked a fresh mag into his Mk12 SPR, the metallic *click* echoing like a promise. His eyes scanned the rifle, checking optics, sling tension, chamber—every inch was second nature by now. Then came the Glock 20, heavier than most sidearms, but an absolute must given what they hunt. He racked the slide, chambered a round, and holstered it with a quiet finality. One long breath in. No words.

Valkyrie double-checked her SCAR-H before sliding an extra FNX-45 Tactical magazine into her vest. She wasn't expecting to use her sidearm, but she wasn't about to be caught unprepared.

Across the room, Diesel finished loading a fresh magazine into his SCAR-H, then patted the M320 grenade launcher slung beneath the barrel. A few 40mm HEDP rounds were stashed in his belt pouches—standard issue, dual-purpose, designed to punch through cover and frag whatever was behind it. His Glock 20 was strapped to his thigh, the grip worn from long use.

Reaper stood near the far wall, tall and lean with a buzz cut and eyes like cold stone. His Knight's Armament M110 SASS was already slung and loaded. He adjusted the suppressor, his movements calm and exact. A Glock 20 rode in a shoulder holster beneath his plate carrier.

Whisper barely glanced up from his drone controller, his fingers moving with eerie precision. "Drones are set for manual and autonomous recon. Thermal and sound suppression activated. We'll deploy them once we reach the lake."

Jonah nodded toward the crate near the door. "C4?"

"Loaded and ready," Diesel said, patting one of the cases. "Timed charges are set to detonate on command or when we need a distraction."

"That leaves the thermal cloaks," Reaper said, passing them out. The specialized fabric was designed to mask their heat signatures, making them invisible to thermal optics and infrared tracking.

Breaker slid his over his shoulders, adjusting the fit. "These never get any more comfortable."

"You want comfort, go back to civilian life," Valkyrie said, clipping hers into place.

No one laughed.

Wildcat knelt near the gear cases, her lean frame coiled with quiet energy. Dark hair was pulled back in a tight braid, and her sharp eyes scanned each weapon with surgical focus. She loaded her SCAR-H with 7.62x51mm armor-piercing rounds, then chambered a round with a clean, practiced motion. Her Glock 20 rested beside her, already loaded with 10mm armor-piercing rounds. When it came to close-quarters or open terrain, Wildcat was always ready.

Jonah took one last look at his team. Fully geared. Focused. Weapons locked and loaded.

This was it.

"Mount up," he said.

Without hesitation, the team moved, grabbing their gear and heading for the Suburbans parked outside. The air was the kind of cold that signaled winter was closing in fast. Their breath came out in short clouds as they loaded their weapons into the back, ensuring everything was secured but easy to access.

Jonah climbed into the Suburban towing the boat trailer, after storing his weapons. The reality of what they were about to do settled in his chest, but he pushed it aside. There was no room for doubt.

Rook jumped into the driver's seat of the lead vehicle, plugging the coordinates into the GPS. Devil's Track Lake boat ramp. The extraction point was set. The route was mapped. Lean and wiry, with close-cropped hair and quick, precise movements, Rook had the focused intensity of someone who lived behind screens but was equally comfortable out in the field.

Havoc slid into the passenger seat, "Gotta love a quiet drive before the chaos."

No one responded.

The rest of the team climbed in, securing their gear between their seats. The mood inside the vehicles was quiet, everyone mentally preparing for the night ahead.

Jonah sat in the second Suburban, staring out the windshield. The glow of the GPS reflected in his eyes, but he wasn't really looking at it. He was going over the plan, every move, every contingency, every worst-case scenario.

So was everyone else.

Without a word, Rook started the engine. The headlights cut through the dark, illuminating the gravel road ahead.

The second vehicle followed.

Slowly, steadily, Echo Black rolled out, heading toward the unknown.

Tonight, they weren't just hunters.

They were heading into enemy territory.

CHAPTER 20

ECHO BLACK

As the Suburbans turned onto the narrow service road leading to Devil's Track Lake, the lead headlights caught the glint of metal, a large gate blocking the path ahead. A rusted sign bolted to the bars read: **GOV. RESTRICTED AREA — FINES WILL APPLY**. Rook brought the first vehicle to a stop, and Jonah pulled up close behind him. The team didn't need to speak.

Diesel stepped out, bolt cutters already in hand. With a heavy clack, the lock snapped clean, falling into the dirt. He swung the gate open wide, and both SUVs rolled through in silence. Once they were clear, Diesel closed the gate behind them, leaving the broken lock dangling.

Five miles later, just before the turnoff to the boat ramp, the two Suburbans killed their headlights, the forest swallowing them in darkness. They coasted the final stretch in silence, tires crunching over gravel.

The vehicles rolled to a stop at the water's edge, with Jonah backing the trailer in. Beyond the lot, Devil's Track Lake stretched wide and still, its surface broken only by faint ripples from the evening breeze. The distant treeline stood as an unbroken wall of black, concealing what waited beyond.

The team moved with silent efficiency, stepping out, eyes focused looking for any movement. The wind blowing off the lake held a sharp bite, but they had worked in worse conditions. Forty-two degrees wasn't cold enough to matter.

No one spoke. No need. They had done this before.

While Havoc and Breaker unstrapped the boat from the trailer, Whisper moved to the back of the Suburban, unzipping a hard case. Inside, a high-end military-grade recon drone rested in its docking station. He activated it, fingers moving over the tablet screen as the machine lifted off. Its rotors spun smoothly, nearly silent, as it rose into the night.

The onboard thermal and night-vision feeds linked directly to Whisper's screen.

He guided the drone toward the far shoreline, running a full sweep of the area.

The sanctuary entrance appeared, the rocky enclave hidden beneath layers of brush and jagged stone. Near the mouth of the cave, two sentinels stood motionless, their enormous heat signatures glowing against the cold rock.

Another stood further back on the narrow trail leading up to the sanctuary, positioned on the opposite side of the lake.

A forth perched on the cliff above the cave, unmoving as it watched the forest below.

Whisper adjusted the drone's flight path, pushing deeper into the wilderness. His screen flared with heat signatures about four miles past the sanctuary.

"Ten of them," he said. "Out hunting, it seems."

Jonah gave a slow nod. That was their opening.

Whisper kept the drone circling the area, running continuous surveillance. It would provide real-time updates, tracking both the hunting group and any activity close to the sanctuary.

"No movement near the lake," he confirmed. "We're clear to go."

Weapons came first.

The team fanned out along the gravel, moving efficiently. Magazines were seated with solid clicks, chambers checked, optics adjusted. Suppressors were secured, sidearms holstered, blades double-checked.

No one spoke.

Valkyrie tapped the side of her scope, Reaper adjusted his sling, and Diesel looked over his rifle one last time. He checked the incendiary 40mm rounds tucked into the elastic pouches along his beltline, each one snug and ready.

Breaker ran a hand across the grenade pouches on his chest rig, feeling the solid weight of the HE rounds locked in place—each one a controlled burst of hell waiting to be launched.

Wildcat's fingers moved fast over her gear, precise and calm.

Whisper didn't look up from the drone feed. His sidearm was secure, and his SCAR-H within reach.

Rook checked the sights on his weapon, steady and focused. Havoc slung his LAMG with casual ease, the belt-fed beast resting comfortably against his chest, while a hatchet rode low on his hip.

Jonah stood watching them all.

In under thirty seconds, nine operators were locked in, ready to move.

Jonah took a step forward.

"Blackout."

The team formed a tight circle, standing shoulder to shoulder. No words. No sound.

Each placed their right hand over their left fist, control over chaos.

For twenty seconds, no-one moved.

Each carried their own thoughts. Some prayed. Some thought of the ones they had lost. Some emptied their minds completely.

Tonight, they all remembered Mason.

He had died twelve months ago on a mission in northern Alaska, ambushed by a 10-foot sasquatch. The moment was brief, but the silence was for him.

When the time passed, Jonah lifted his hands and clapped his knuckles together.

A single jagged sound.

The circle broke.

The mission was on.

Havoc and Diesel moved first, stepping into the shallows and gripping the hull. Breaker moved to the trailer, released the winch, and unhooked the safety chain. With a nod from Jonah, they gave the hull a solid shove. The boat slid smoothly off the trailer and into the water, settling with a low splash as it rocked into place

One by one, the team climbed in, keeping low. Their weapons and gear settled into place as they took position.

Breaker fired up the engine. The quiet hum barely carried over the water as they pushed off, gliding out onto the lake.

The first stretch went fast. The boat cut through the dark water, moving with controlled speed toward the old dock.

Jonah sat near the stern, eyes fixed ahead. The treeline was getting closer, the shadows stretching taller.

Halfway across, Breaker turned down the revs to the lowest idle and crept slowly towards the dock.

No one moved. Weapons stayed raised, eyes scanning the shoreline.

Whisper lifted his tablet, watching the drone feed in

real-time. He exhaled through his nose.

"They haven't moved," he murmured. "Two still at the cave. One on the trail. One on the cliff above."

The boat glided closer, the treeline expanding ahead.

Jonah nodded, keeping his voice low. "The hunters?"

"Still four miles out," Whisper confirmed. "Looks like they're stalking deer."

Jonah glanced at the others. That gave them time.

Then Whisper frowned slightly, eyes narrowing at his screen.

"Rob's still there," he said, voice quiet. "But his heat signature's weak."

A beat of silence.

"Poor guy must be freezing," Valkyrie said.

Breaker adjusted his grip on the wheel. "Rest of them must be in the cave."

CHAPTER 21

SASQUATCH HUNTERS

The forest pulsed with life, but the Sasquatch stood still, waiting.

Aluk crouched low near the edge of a narrow game trail, pressing his massive fingers into the damp earth. The scent of deer was strong in the air. A large herd was moving. Their direction had already shifted.

Matto stood to his left, half-shadowed by a fallen pine, still as stone. Tahkan waited just ahead, crouched at the trail's edge, muscles taut with anticipation. The youngest of the three, his tension was visible in the slow shift of his stance, the way his fingers flexed near the dirt.

They were the end of the funnel, the final block in a carefully laid trap.

Behind them, the terrain opened into rough elevation and thick brush. Ahead, the winding trail narrowed through stone and root, channeling everything toward this point.

The rest of the hunting party had already begun, spread wide through the woods. Their task was simple: drive the herd this way. Push them, guide them, contain them until they ran straight into the waiting jaws of their own extinction.

Matto scanned the brush without turning his head, slow breaths misting faintly in the cold. Tahkan remained low, eyes locked forward. No one moved.

Aluk didn't need to signal. The plan was already in motion. The herd wouldn't see them until it was far too late.

A gust of wind stirred the treetops. Hoofbeats echoed faintly through the trees.

Aluk rose to his full height, colossal and silent.

The trap was closing.

CHAPTER 22

ECHO BLACK

The speedboat glided through the darkness, moving stealthily toward the ragged wooden dock jutting out from the shoreline. The structure was old, weathered by years of neglect, but still standing. It creaked slightly as the boat neared, the gentle lapping of water against its supports the only sound in the stillness of the night.

Breaker barely moved, keeping his hands light on the wheel as he adjusted their course. The distant treeline loomed ahead, a jagged silhouette against the sky. Beyond the dock, the shoreline stretched—a rough mix of sand, mud, and scattered rocks leading up toward the forest.

A steady breeze drifted across the lake, cool and constant, scented with damp rot, pine sap and a trace of something not meant to be there. No sounds beyond the rustling of distant leaves and the occasional ripple of water against the hull.

Jonah scanned the shoreline through his night-vision, then tapped his earpiece. "Whisper, anything?"

"Sentinels haven't moved," Whisper said, his voice quiet in their comms. "Two at the cave entrance. One on the trail. One above the cave. No changes."

Jonah gave a single nod. That was what they needed to hear.

They were twenty yards from the dock when Diesel leaned over, gripping the coiled rope. The boat drifted silently into position.

Diesel tossed the mooring line around one of the sturdier-looking dock posts. The wood groaned under the weight but held.

Jonah lifted his hand. Move.

The team stepped onto the dock one by one, their boots landing lightly on the worn planks. The wood flexed under their weight but didn't give. Once all were ashore, they slipped onto the shoreline beyond. Whisper stayed on the boat to monitor the drone feeds.

They had a long walk ahead of them.

Four hundred and fifty yards along the shoreline stood between them and the point where they'd turn north through the ravine, into the forest.

The first few steps sank into damp sand, the lake lapping softly at the edges. Further up, the terrain shifted to a thick mess of mud, jagged river rocks and exposed roots, forcing them to move with careful steps. Driftwood lay scattered across the bank, half-buried in the sand, remnants of past storms.

Breaker mumbled under his breath as he stumbled slightly on a loose rock. "Hell of a walk just to get to the start line."

"Try not to break your ankle before we even get there," Valkyrie whispered back.

Jonah ignored the exchange, keeping his eyes ahead. The treeline was close, too close for a Sasquatch to surprise them.

When they reached the point where they needed to turn north, Jonah raised a fist, signaling a halt.

Ahead of them, the forest thickened, and the terrain sloped downward sharply.

A natural obstacle lay ahead, a ravine cutting through the landscape, roughly 20 feet deep.

Rook and Valkyrie moved up, crouching beside a thick fallen tree that had partially collapsed into the ravine. They scanned ahead.

Valkyrie turned slightly, her voice barely above a breath. "We can go around, but it'll take time."

Jonah assessed the terrain. They could divert left and take an extra few minutes, but time wasn't a luxury.

He nodded. "We go fast. Low. One at a time. No noise."

They moved.

One by one, they descended carefully into the ravine, boots sliding slightly against the damp, rocky earth. The incline was steep but manageable, loose soil shifting beneath their weight. At the bottom, the ground leveled out briefly before sloping upward again on the opposite side.

Jonah took the lead up the opposite bank, using exposed roots for leverage. One by one, they followed.

As he reached the treeline on the other side, Whisper's voice came through.

"Still no movement," he murmured. "You're clear."

They pushed on.

The terrain began to slope upward, signaling they were getting close. The rocks here were jagged and slick, remnants of an old landslide. It forced them to slow their pace, navigating carefully over uneven footing.

Whisper's voice came through again, low and steady.

"Rob's heat signature still there. Weak."

Jonah's focus intensified as they pressed forward.

They were less than two hundred yards out when Whisper's voice changed slightly.

"Hold up."

Everyone froze.

Jonah lowered himself into a crouch, back pressing against the rough bark of a pine. The others mirrored his movement, sinking into the darkness, weapons raised.

"Talk to me," Jonah whispered.

"New heat signature just showed up."

Jonah's grip on his rifle tightened. "Where?"

"Right behind Rob," Whisper said. "It just walked up."

Silence settled over the group.

Breaker adjusted his stance, his gaze locked on the treeline ahead. "Size?"

Whisper hesitated. "Much smaller than the hunting group's signatures. Could be a young'un."

Jonah's mind worked fast.

The team stayed frozen in place. The steady wind shifted slightly, rustling the trees overhead.

Rob wasn't alone anymore.

****

Jonah and the team remained low, motionless against the trees, their weapons steady. No one moved. No one even shifted their weight. They had been trained to hold still for long periods, even when every nerve screamed for action.

Whisper's voice came through their comms, quiet but focused.

"It's still there. The young'un."

"It's crouching next to him now," Whisper continued. "Looks like... yeah. It's giving him something."

Jonah's grip on his SCAR-H tightened slightly. "What?"

"Hard to tell," Whisper murmured. "Wait... okay, Rob's reaching for it. Drinking something."

Wildcat shifted slightly, barely tilting her head. "Shit. Kid's keeping him alive."

Jonah didn't respond immediately. His focus remained on the dense forest ahead. The cave entrance was still nearly two hundred yards away, but every step closer meant greater risk.

"How much time before the others are back?" Jonah asked.

There was a brief pause before Whisper responded, his voice more urgent now. "Shit, hold up."

Jonah's spine stiffened. "Talk."

Whisper's fingers flew across his controls as the drone feed adjusted. "The hunting group just accelerated. Fast."

"Define fast," Valkyrie said.

"They were stalking before. Slow and methodical. Now? They just took down three deer." Whisper's voice carried a new edge. "They're moving different, aggressive. Like they're wrapping things up."

Jonah's mind worked fast. That meant one thing.

"They'll be heading back soon," Whisper confirmed.

No one needed to say what that meant.

If they didn't reach Rob and extract him now, they wouldn't make it out before the hunting group arrived.

Jonah exhaled through his nose. "No more delays. We go now."

He tapped his earpiece. "Tell me what the young'un is doing now."

Whisper adjusted the drone's altitude slightly. "Still next to him. Not leaving. Looks like it's just watching him now."

Valkyrie breathed out, steady and controlled. "Can't wait for it to move. Could stay there all night."

Diesel grunted quietly. "So what? We still going?"

Jonah didn't hesitate. "Yeah. We go."

No more waiting.

With the hunting group's return approaching, their time was running out.

Jonah looked to Reaper. "When we're in range, take out

the cliff sentinel before he spots us."

"Got it," Reaper confirmed.

Jonah touched his earpiece. "Whisper, keep tracking the hunters. The second they turn back, I want to know."

"Understood."

Jonah lifted his hand in a tight signal. Go.

The team moved.

CHAPTER 23

SASQUATCH HUNTERS

Aluk crouched low near the trail, nostrils flaring. Tahkan and Matto waited behind him, still and alert. The others were already in motion, spread wide through the forest, sweeping inward in a silent arc. The herd had only one way to run.

The terrain had been chosen carefully. Steep rock flanked one side of the forest, and dense underbrush choked the other. Only a single narrow trail cut through the middle, and that was where the trap had been set.

The wind shifted.

In the distance, a branch snapped. Then another.

The herd began to move.

Aluk's posture shifted. The trap had sprung.

The first of the deer burst into the clearing, eyes wide with panic, hooves hammering the earth. More followed in a frantic blur of limbs and instinct.

Tahkan moved first, lunging from the treeline. He didn't need to strike. His presence alone was enough to drive the animals deeper down the trail.

Matto was already waiting.

A large buck veered left, attempting to break from the path.

Matto intercepted, massive arms lashing out. He crashed into the buck's flank, wrapping it in a crushing grip. With a brutal twist, he snapped the spine. The animal dropped without a sound.

To the right, Tahkan redirected a smaller doe into the final gap, where one of the elder males stepped forward and brought it down with a single, devastating blow.

The scent of blood flooded the air.

But Aluk wasn't done.

Ahead, one last buck bolted for the treeline, slower than the rest.

Aluk gave chase.

The forest blurred around him. Every step was precise. Every motion lethal. Trees, brush and moonlight streaked past as he gained ground.

The buck leapt a fallen tree.

Aluk leapt with it.

He collided mid-air, his arms wrapping around the animal's chest and dragging it down hard. The buck hit the ground thrashing, hooves kicking wildly.

Aluk clamped down, pinning it to the earth. His jaws closed over its throat.

The buck spasmed once. Twice.

Then it was still.

Aluk rose slowly, chest heaving. The warmth of the fresh kill soaked into his fingers. Around him, the others were gathering, emerging from the trees with their own kills in tow.

Matto appeared first, blood wet on his hands. He dropped his buck beside Aluk's and exhaled, steady and satisfied.

Tahkan followed, stepping lightly, his eyes scanning the

edge of the trees.

For a moment, all was still.

The only sounds were wind through the branches and the distant stir of smaller creatures retreating.

Without a word, Aluk turned from the kill and looked back toward the direction of the sanctuary.

The hunt was complete.

CHAPTER 24

ECHO BLACK

Jonah and the team moved with careful precision, slipping between the trees like ghosts. Boots pressed lightly into the damp earth. No branches cracked, no gear rattled. Every movement was controlled, deliberate. They were less than thirty yards from Rob, hidden beneath layers of shadow and thick foliage.

The small Sasquatch crouched beside Rob, his small frame tight with tension. His nostrils flared. He lifted his head, wide amber eyes scanning the darkness. Something was wrong.

Jonah froze mid-step and raised a closed fist. The team halted instantly.

The small Sasquatch's ears twitched. His breathing quickened.

Then, a low, grating growl rolled from his throat. Not aggressive. Not a challenge.

Fear.

Then he bolted.

Rob flinched at the movement, but his mind barely reacted. The cold had drained him of everything—thought, strength, will. He blinked slowly, barely processing as the young Sasquatch vanished toward the cave.

Jonah's stomach dropped.

They had seconds.

A shadow shifted above.

Reaper's voice came over comms, low and calm. "Sentinel on the cliff just clocked us."

Jonah didn't hesitate. "Take him."

The suppressed crack of Reaper's M110 SASS cut through the stillness.

The sentinel crumpled.

The body didn't tumble. It plummeted.

It hit the ground in front of the cave with a sickening,

bone-snapping thud.

The two sentinels posted at the cave entrance turned at the sound. Their enormous frames went rigid.

Then they looked up.

Their eyes locked on Echo Black.

A single beat of silence.

Then the screaming began.

It hit like a wall. Layered howls and screeches shredded the air. Deep, throaty bellows filled the clearing with a primal dissonance meant to disorient and paralyze.

Jonah's ears rang. He gritted his teeth and powered through it.

Rook hunched his shoulders, blinking rapidly. "Jesus Christ…"

"Hit them!" Jonah barked.

Breaker dropped to a knee, pulled a 40mm HE round from his chest rig, and loaded it into the M320 grenade launcher slung beneath his SCAR-H. One clean motion.

He fired.

The grenade exploded just in front of the cave.

The nearest sentinel was torn apart, the blast shredding through its chest in a burst of blood and bone.

The second was thrown into the stone wall, twitching, one leg bent unnaturally.

Further down the trail, the fourth sentinel staggered from the treeline, dazed but on its feet.

"Go!" Jonah shouted.

Rook and Valkyrie sprinted for Rob.

Rook dropped beside him and sliced through the vine bindings with his combat knife. Rob sagged into him, limp.

Valkyrie grabbed under Rob's arms. "You with me?" Rob's lips moved, but no sound came.

"We've gotta carry him," Rook said, slinging Rob's arm over his shoulder.

Valkyrie did the same, and together, they started dragging him toward the treeline.

Jonah turned back toward the cave.

The grenade blast had bought them seconds. Nothing

more.

The sentinel that had hit the wall was staggering upright, bleeding and furious.

Down the trail, the fourth sentinel let out a bellow and charged.

From deep inside the cave, a low, subterranean growl rumbled out. It vibrated through the ground and up through their boots. Not rage. Not hunger.

A summons.

Jonah ordered his team forward. "Move. Now."

Valkyrie and Rook hauled Rob forward, his dead weight dragging behind them. Echo Black closed formation, weapons up, covering the retreat.

The first surviving sentinel hissed and charged.

The last followed, gaining ground with long strides.

"Drop them!" Jonah ordered.

The clearing erupted.

Breaker's SCAR-H barked three times. His shots tore into the first sentinel's chest and shoulder, slowing it but not stopping it.

Diesel stepped forward, keeping his SCAR-H tight to his shoulder. He fired short, controlled bursts. One round slammed through the creature's collarbone, another into its lower jaw. The third hit center mass.

The sentinel collapsed mid-stride and skidded across the dirt, lifeless.

The fourth was already on them.

Wildcat pivoted fast, the hulking swing barely missing her head. From a crouch, she drove a Karambit upward into its jaw. The blade sank deep. The creature recoiled, howling.

A suppressed shot rang out.

Reaper's M110 SASS punched a round through its skull.

It dropped instantly.

Jonah scanned the treeline. No movement.

The sentinels were down.

Then, from within the cave, the growl came again. Deeper this time. Closer.

"More incoming," Jonah said.

Whisper's voice crackled over comms. "Confirmed. Seven heat signatures moving toward the entrance. Big ones."

Jonah turned to the team. "Get him moving. We don't have long."

Rook and Valkyrie adjusted their grip on Rob and picked up the pace. His feet barely touched the ground as they dragged him through the forest.

Then came the first shape in the cave.

The Elder.

Still. Watching.

Behind him, more figures moved in the dark.

Jonah's heart pounded.

They weren't just fighting to escape anymore.

This was war.

He looked back once.

Then turned forward.

"We run."

CHAPTER 25

SASQUATCH HUNTERS

Aluk moved at the front of the hunting party, his body loose, his thoughts steady. Behind him, the others carried their kills, their breathing deep and satisfied. The weight of fresh meat pressed against their backs, but it was a welcome weight. Strength. Success.

Matto slung a hefty buck over his shoulder, fingers still damp with warmth. Tahkan walked beside him, his restless energy still thrumming despite the night's effort. The rest followed, moving in pairs, thick bodies weaving between the trees.

They stopped at a spring-fed creek, where the water ran cold and clear.

Matto dropped his buck beside the bank and crouched low, dipping his hands into the stream. The rest followed, drinking deeply, their heavy exhales stirring the water's surface.

Aluk scooped a handful, cooling his throat. The hunt had been long, but the blood on his hands was good.

Matto grunted. *"Strong hunt."*

Aluk chuffed low in agreement. *"Yes."*

Tahkan flicked water from his fingers, his restless energy still buzzing. *"Almost lost mine in the rocks."*

Matto huffed, baring his teeth slightly. *"Then be faster."*

Tahkan let out a sharp chattering click, not quite playful.

He stayed tense. He let out a quick burst of clipped grunts, followed by quick chattering hum. His hands made a small flick, reinforcing what had already been said.

"The Elder had spoken. The hairless one must end. Tonight."

Aluk turned his head, his eyes narrowing. He replied with a single, flat grunt.

"So?"

Tahkan responded, faster this time. His chatter was louder, more urgent. His fingers slashed once through the air.

"Why did you spare him? The others were ended."

Aluk growled low and deep. One hand opened, then slowly closed into a fist.

"More would come. For him. We will end them too."

Matto shifted. His breath came hard and hot. He let out a long grunt and tapped his chest, then motioned toward the forest. His hand mimicked the crack of a thunder stick.

A pause. Then a slow grunts.

"They may end some of clan with thunder sticks."

Aluk scoffed. His answer came with a long exhale and a low grunt. His shoulders rolled in dismissal. He did not care.

Tahkan hesitated. Then softer grunts.

"What if they don't come?"

Aluk rose to his full height. He said nothing at first. Then came the rumble. Deep. Final.

"Then we go to them."

Images followed: Hairless ones running. Their dens burning. Their metal machines crumbled.

Matto made no sound. He simply watched the trees.

Tahkan nodded. No more questions.

Then the night shattered.

The war cry ripped through the trees.

Three voices. Together.

A piercing scream. A deep roar. A bone-shaking howl.

Aluk's head snapped up. Ears forward.

The hunting party froze.

No movement. No breath.

The sentinels only screamed together if the sanctuary was under attack.

Then the second sound.

Thunder sticks clapping.

Deep. Unnatural.

Wrong.

Aluk's body went tight. Muscles ready.

Matto exhaled sharply, nostrils flaring.

Tahkan growled. *"Hairless ones."*

Aluk grunted low in his throat. Short. Hard. Commanding.

"Drop the kills."

Matto didn't wait. He let the buck slide from his shoulders, its weight hitting the dirt with a dull thud.

The others followed. Meat didn't matter now.

Another grunt. Lower. Rolling. Urgent.

"Move."

As they surged forward, Aluk threw his head back and roared.

The sound ripped through the trees, deep and powerful, shaking the branches. It was an answer. A signal.

The sentinels would hear.

They would know.

The hunters were coming.

Massive bodies surged forward, crashing through the trees. Fast. Silent. Powerful.

The sanctuary was four miles away.

They would be there before the hairless ones could escape.

They would rip. Tear. Crush.

The hairless ones thought they could spill blood and leave.

They were wrong.

CHAPTER 26

ECHO BLACK

Jonah kept his SCAR-H raised, eyes sweeping the darkness behind as his team dragged Rob between them, pushing toward the treeline. Their boots pounded the earth, breath misting in the cold night air.

Behind them, the cave erupted with movement.

The Elder had barely registered what had happened before the first of the Sasquatch burst from the entrance. Huge, dark figures streamed into the open, fast and terrifyingly quiet for their size.

"Move fast," Whisper's voice hissed over comms from the drone feed. "You've got a horde pouring out of that cave, and the hunting party's running back full-speed. They'll be on you soon."

Jonah's stomach knotted. They had a long way back to the boat.

"Copy," he said. "Reaper, hit what you see."

The sniper didn't hesitate. A single, suppressed crack echoed faintly through the trees. One of the charging Sasquatch dropped, tumbling face-first into the earth.

The others didn't slow.

Gunfire erupted behind Jonah.

Diesel fired in controlled bursts with his SCAR-H, armor-piercing rounds slamming into thick bodies. Beside him, Havoc let his Knight's Armament LAMG thunder, 7.62mm rounds tearing through hide and bone. Two more creatures collapsed under the barrage, but the rest vaulted over the dead and kept coming.

Jonah's SCAR-H barked. Controlled bursts. Center mass. Still they advanced.

The Elder remained near the cave, unmoving. Watching. Letting his kin do the work.

"Go, go, go!" Jonah shouted.

Valkyrie and Rook dragged Rob between them, dragging his half-limp body forward.

"We've got him," Rook grunted, shifting more of Rob's weight over his shoulder. "Just keep us covered!"

"Reaper, keep thinning the pack," Jonah ordered.

"Working on it," came Reaper's calm reply.

Another shot. Another Sasquatch dropped.

But it wasn't enough.

The hunting party reached the sanctuary, their arrival announced by a deafening cacophony of overlapping roars.

The sound vibrated through their chests.

Jonah risked a glance back.

Tree limbs cracked in the distance.

"Shit," Breaker growled. "They're fast."

Whisper came over comms again. "They're closing in. You've got less than a minute."

Jonah didn't hesitate. "Keep moving!"

Diesel and Havoc pivoted, laying down covering fire. Diesel's rounds dropped one mid-stride. Havoc's belt-fed LAMG shredded another, tearing its thigh open and sending it tumbling.

Still more came.

Jonah gritted his teeth. Too many. Too close.

"Breaker!" Jonah barked. "HE round—now!"

Breaker skidded to a stop, pulled a 40mm HE grenade from the front pouch of his vest, and loaded it into the M320 under his SCAR-H. He fired.

The grenade exploded mid pack. Several of the charging Sasquatch dropped, flailing. Others recoiled, dazed and staggering.

But not all of them.

Aluk barely slowed.

Jonah's pulse spiked.

The big one was still coming. Matto followed, rage in every movement.

Aluk let out a low grunt, and the others shifted formation, spreading wide.

They were herding Echo Black toward the lake.

Jonah made a split-second call.

"Diesel, take Wildcat and flank left! Reaper, cover their

path!"

Diesel grabbed Wildcat's arm and pulled her into the trees. If they could split the pursuit, they had a chance.

For a second, it worked.

Until Matto spotted them.

A harsh series of clicks and snarls spilled from his throat, commands.

Two Sasquatch broke off and charged into the woods.

Reaper shifted, sighted, and fired. The M110 SASS barked once. A round punched through the spine of the nearest creature. It dropped instantly.

The second reached them.

Wildcat rolled under its swing and slashed upward, cutting a deep line across its chest with her Karambit. It shrieked and lunged again.

Diesel fired two shots into its shoulder and chest, then stepped forward and fired once more into its face.

It dropped.

"Clear," Diesel barked. They moved again, fast and low.

Back with the main group, Whisper's voice cut in.

"Sending help. One drone inbound."

A soft whir rose above them.

The recon drone swept overhead, twin-mounted mini-guns rotating and locking onto targets.

It opened fire.

The tree line exploded in noise and flying bark. Sasquatch fell under the barrage, screaming as rounds shredded branches and bodies.

Some slowed. Some stopped.

It wasn't much, but it was enough.

"Move!" Jonah shouted. "Now!"

The team surged forward.

Then Breaker went down.

His boot caught a root, and he crashed hard, a jagged branch stabbing clean through his forearm. He screamed.

"Shit!" Valkyrie dropped Rob and dropped to Breaker's side. The branch was embedded deep, blood streaming out.

"Fuuuck," he hissed, face contorted.

"Hold still," she snapped.

"No time. Do it," Breaker said through gritted teeth.

She braced her foot and yanked. The branch came free. Breaker screamed, then staggered to his feet, clutching the wound.

Jonah turned just in time to see Aluk break the treeline, barreling toward them, trees snapping in his path.

Jonah pulled a frag grenade, yanked the pin.

"Cover your ears!"

He threw it.

The grenade bounced twice and detonated, shrapnel and heat erupting through the darkness.

Two pursuers dropped. Aluk recoiled and changed direction.

Five more seconds.

That was all they needed.

They ran.

The ravine loomed ahead.

And beyond it, the lake.

CHAPTER 27

The treeline thinned ahead. The ravine was just yards away.

Rook sprinted forward, dragging Rob's nearly limp body with Valkyrie. His lungs burned, muscles screaming under the weight. Rob sagged between them, half-conscious, barely able to move.

Then the first Sasquatch hit.

Tahkan came from the right, a blur of muscle and matted hair. He slammed into Rook like a wrecking ball, sending all three crashing into the dirt.

Rob tumbled free, rolling across the ground.

Pain shot through Rook's ribs and shoulder. He barely

had time to react before Tahkan's enormous hand came down.

Rook threw up his SCAR-H, bracing the rifle between them.

Metal met flesh. The creature's nails scraped across the upper receiver, jarring the weapon in Rook's hands.

Tahkan snarled in his face, breath hot and sour.

Rook drove a knee into the beast's gut, but it barely flinched.

Then came the first shot.

A sharp crack rang through the trees as Valkyrie fired. Her SCAR-H spat a single armor-piercing round that tore through Tahkan's shoulder in a mist of blood.

The Sasquatch staggered.

From the left, Diesel moved in. His SCAR-H kicked hard against his shoulder as he fired a short burst. The first round tore into Tahkan's side. The second punched through the lower ribs and exited clean.

Havoc wasn't far behind. His Knight's Armament LAMG thundered, 7.62mm rounds slamming into Tahkan's chest and sternum, driving him back.

Then Wildcat moved.

Fast. Silent.

She leapt onto Tahkan's back, one Karambit already in hand. She buried the curved blade into the side of his neck, twisting hard.

Her second blade dropped into his right eye.

The sound he made was somewhere between a roar and a choke.

He jerked once. Convulsed.

Then dropped.

Wildcat rolled off before the body hit the ground, blades dripping, chest heaving. "One down," she said.

No time to breathe.

Matto crashed through the trees, charging toward them.

"Pick him up!" Jonah barked, pointing to Rob.

Havoc took over for Rook, dropping to one knee and hauled Rob upright, muscles straining under the weight. Valkyrie grabbed the other side, helping him move.

Jonah covered their six, SCAR-H firing in controlled

bursts.

The ravine was ahead.

They were out of time.

CHAPTER 28

ECHO BLACK

Jonah pushed forward, rifle raised as the team sprinted toward the ravine. Tahkan's corpse lay behind them, his blood steaming in the cold night air, but Matto and the others didn't stop. If anything, they came harder.

Whisper's voice cut through the comms.

"Jonah, you've got three closing in fast. Aluk's leading them."

Jonah already heard them. The pounding of hefty feet.

The heavy breath of something in pursuit.

The ravine was only thirty yards away.

A blur of movement to his left.

One of the Sasquatch lunged.

Jonah twisted, barely clearing the swipe. A gigantic hand sliced through the air where his head had been. Wind from the strike whipped across his face. He fired point-blank.

The SCAR-H barked.

The first two rounds punched through the creature's ribs. The third ripped through its throat. Staggering, the Sasquatch hit the ground on its knees, clutching its neck as blood poured between its fingers.

Jonah didn't stop to watch it die.

Diesel wasn't as lucky.

A Sasquatch slammed into his back, driving him into the dirt with brutal force. Diesel grunted as he hit hard, his SCAR-H skidding away. The beast loomed over him, snarling, its mouth wet with saliva.

It raised a monstrous fist.

Then came two cracks.

The creature's head snapped sideways. Its jaw shattered, teeth exploding as Glock 20 armor-piercing rounds tore half its face off.

Diesel shoved up from the dirt and fired again, straight through its open mouth.

"Ugly bastard," he muttered, blood and brain matter spraying the brush.

Rook grabbed Diesel's vest and hauled him up.

"Get moving. We don't have time."

They reached the ravine.

"Get across. Now."

Wildcat replaced Valkyrie, helping Havoc carry Rob down the slope. The others followed, boots skidding on loose rock.

Rook turned, laying down suppressing fire. His SCAR-H shredded the legs out from under the nearest Sasquatch, chunks of flesh and hair spraying the rocks.

A low, rumbling growl.

Jonah turned and saw Aluk barreling toward them. He moved faster than anything that size should.

He didn't stop. He leapt.

Jonah dove to the side as Aluk landed on the ravine's

edge. Dust and stone exploded underfoot.

For a split-second, their eyes met.

No hesitation. No fear.

Aluk charged.

Jonah fired. Rounds slammed into the creature's hip. It didn't slow.

A huge arm swung.

Jonah barely braced before it connected.

The impact sent his world spinning white.

He was airborne.

He crashed into the rocks below. Pain lit up his ribs. He rolled onto his side, gasping, scrambling for his rifle.

Aluk was already coming.

Jonah raised his SCAR-H, finger tightening on the trigger.

Gunfire slammed into Aluk's shoulder, forcing him to veer off.

Jonah wasn't the one who fired.

Reaper stood at the edge of the ravine, his M110 SASS smoking.

"Get up, Ghost."

Jonah didn't need to be told twice. He forced himself upright, ribs screaming.

Behind Reaper, the team was already across.

Only he and Rook were still exposed.

Rook dropped another mag into his SCAR-H and fired at a charging target.

"We're getting pinned, boss."

Jonah slapped a fresh magazine into his own rifle and turned.

With his good arm, Breaker was setting charges along the loose rock face.

He didn't need to ask what the plan was.

"Move!" Jonah shouted.

Rook covered him as they ran.

The moment their boots hit the far side of the ravine, Breaker triggered the C4.

The blast ripped through the canyon wall. Rock and dirt exploded upward in a thunderous wave. Mid-crossing creatures vanished into the debris.

When the smoke cleared, one of them was still moving.

It stumbled forward, arms gone, blown off at the shoulder. It didn't seem to realize.

Blood sprayed from both stumps. The thing took three more steps.

Then it collapsed.

A twitch. A final, choked breath.

Stillness.

Jonah exhaled, heart pounding.

They had made it across.

CHAPTER 29

ECHO BLACK

Jonah wiped sweat and dirt from his face, chest heaving as he stared at the unmoving body of the armless Sasquatch. The thing had run for nearly five full seconds after losing its limbs, its massive frame twitching before finally succumbing to blood loss.

It was dead.

But the fight was far from over.

"Status?" Jonah rasped into his comms. His ribs ached, and every breath felt like swallowing broken glass.

Whisper's voice came through from the boat, calm but tense. "Still tracking movement. That blast took out at least eight, but two of the largest signatures are stumbling. Not sure how they're standing."

Jonah looked back across the destroyed ravine. Through drifting smoke and powdered dirt, the remaining two loomed.

One of them stood at the edge, unmoving. His broad chest rose and fell. His posture was still, too still. Thick, matted hair streaked with blood—his or another's—clung to his shoulders. The moonlight caught in his dark eyes.

Jonah knew that look.

This one wasn't finished.

Behind him, another crouched low, knuckles against the rocks. Bulkier. Tense. Ready to charge. It shifted forward, teeth bared, but the lead creature grunted and held out an arm.

The second stopped.

A long silence settled.

Then the leader tilted his head back and released a deep, rasping call.

It rolled through the trees like thunder, echoing into the woods beyond.

Not a cry of pain. Not rage.

A summons.

Jonah's stomach clenched.

"Whisper," he said, forcing calm into his voice. "Tell me you don't see more incoming."

A few long seconds passed.

Then Whisper responded, grim.

"They're coming."

Jonah inhaled deeply.

Valkyrie reloaded her SCAR-H. Armor-piercing rounds slid home with a solid click.

"Then we better not be here when they get here," she said.

Jonah turned and scanned the team.

Breaker's arm was a mangled mess, blood soaked into the sleeve as Valkyrie packed QuikClot gauze over the wound. Diesel stood nearby, shirt torn across the back, revealing a long gash crusted with dried blood. Wildcat's shoulder was slashed open, sticky with Sasquatch blood and her own. She was still on her feet but moving slower now.

Havoc supported Rob under one arm, keeping him upright. Rob trembled beneath Tyson's windbreaker, eyes glassy with cold and pain.

They couldn't take another hit.

Jonah turned again to the ravine. The lead Sasquatch hadn't moved.

Still watching.

Still waiting.

Jonah raised his SCAR-H, sight aligned.

For a moment, they stared at each other across the gap, two hunters gauging the other.

Jonah fired.

The shot cracked through the night.

But the creature was already gone, vanished the instant Jonah pulled the trigger.

Jonah's gut twisted.

"Move. Fast."

The team surged forward, breaking from cover and disappearing into the trees.

CHAPTER 30

THE SASQUATCH

The night air reeked of blood, burned hair, and dust.

Aluk stood at the shattered edge of the ravine, his immense chest rising and falling in slow, steady breaths. The earth beneath him was still warm from the explosion, littered with the broken bodies of his fallen kin. He ignored the sting of raw, blistered skin along his arms, shoulder and back, the harsh scent of his own scorched hair filling his nostrils.

Pain meant nothing.

Aluk roared, a monstrous sound that shook the trees and sent their leaves trembling.

His eyes dropped to the path ahead, where the hairless ones had vanished.

They were running.

Good.

Matto paced beside him, heavy steps crunching over loose rock. His deep-set eyes flicked toward Aluk, then back to the trees, hands clenching and unclenching. Smoke still curled from the tips of his singed hair.

A low, irritated grunt rumbled from Matto's throat, followed by a sharp burst of chattering.

"We go after them now. Before they reach the water."

Aluk didn't respond.

Matto let out a harsher grunt, impatience twisting his already battered face. He shifted, shoulders rolling as if to shake off restraint.

"Aluk, they..."

Aluk turned his head slightly and exhaled a slow, deep breath through his nose. The quiet growl that followed held meaning.

"Wait."

Matto stiffened but said nothing more.

Aluk shifted his gaze to the tree line, listening. The hairless ones had fled quickly, but he could still hear them in the distance. Their footfalls crashed through the underbrush. Their ragged breathing rode the wind. They had lost too much blood. They were slow now.

But their thunder sticks...

Aluk's fingers flexed, the burned skin on his knuckles pulling tight. A deep chuff rumbled from his chest. A memory flared.

A warrior's head torn away in a spray of red, flesh ripped, bones shattered, the stench of fresh wounds wafted in the air.

He projected the image toward Matto.

The warning was clear.

Matto's jaw clenched. His lips curled back from yellowed teeth, but he gave a quick grunt of understanding.

They had underestimated the hairless ones.

Not again.

A distant sound rolled through the trees behind them. Heavy footfalls. A low, harsh chuff echoed in the dark.

The others were coming.

Aluk shifted his gaze to the trail that led back toward the sanctuary. His summons had been heard.

They would not fight alone.

The first figures emerged from the trees, their broad silhouettes washed in moonlight. More warriors. More rage.

A thick-bodied female stepped into view, her dark hair streaked with ash and dirt. Others followed, enormous forms moving through the dark, eyes gleaming with the same fury that simmered in Aluk's chest.

He counted as they arrived.

Seven males. Four females.

The mothers had remained in the sanctuary with the Elder, guarding the young.

But these had come to kill.

Matto's chest heaved. His hands flexed again. He grunted low, chattering.

"Now?"

Aluk exhaled once more and answered with a deep, final

grunt.

"Now."

They wouldn't wait any longer.

They didn't need to.

The hairless ones were fast, but not fast enough.

Aluk sent a final image pulsing through the group: the moonlit trail, the scent of blood, the lake at the edge of the trees, the hairless one's bleeding as they ran.

The message was clear.

Understanding passed between them in silence.

Then they moved as one, across the ravine and into the trees.

CHAPTER 31

ECHO BLACK

The trees exploded as the Sasquatch broke from the forest, their enormous bodies moving with terrifying speed. Some ran upright, huge arms pumping as they closed in. Others dropped to all fours, galloping like monsters from a nightmare.

They didn't just chase now. They hunted. Low to the ground, long arms driving them forward faster than any human could hope to run. Their knuckles gouged deep into the dirt with each stride. Muscular legs taut and sprang like loaded traps.

It was unnatural. No creature that big should move like that.

Jonah glanced back.

"Faster!"

The team pushed harder, bodies failing but refusing to stop.

Jonah skidded to a halt and spun. The team followed, rifles raised.

"Light them up!"

Gunfire shredded the night.

Echo Black unleashed hell. Muzzle flashes lit the dark as high-caliber rounds ripped into the charging Sasquatch. Bullets punched through muscle and shattered bone. Screams and howls rang out across the shoreline.

Some faltered. Some fell. Others kept coming, hair soaked in blood, hate burning in their eyes.

Jonah fired in controlled bursts. His SCAR-H kicked hard as he drove rounds into a Sasquatch's chest. Bone and muscle tore away, but the beast staggered three more steps before it dropped.

A deafening roar rose from the Sasquatch.

Aluk charged at the front, fury in his eyes and no sign of pain slowing him. His legs pounded the ground with shocking speed.

Whisper's voice crackled through comms.

"I see him!"

A beat later, a rifle cracked from the boat.

Aluk saw it coming.

In one smooth motion, he grabbed a nearby female warrior and yanked her in front of him.

The shot hit her center mass. Blood exploded from her back as she let out a strangled cry.

Jonah flinched.

A second round tore through her and struck Aluk in the face, blasting part of his ear off. A spray of red misted the air.

Aluk staggered, blood pouring down his neck and shoulder.

He reached up, touched the torn flesh, and looked at the blood on his hand.

His breathing deepened.

Lips peeled back. Jagged teeth gleamed.

A low growl rose from deep in his chest.

Jonah raised his rifle again, but Aluk dropped low and vanished behind a boulder.

Whisper cursed.

"I lost him!"

The ground trembled.

More Sasquatch surged forward.

Diesel pivoted to fire, but one slammed into him, driving him to the sand.

The beast landed on top, its over-sized hands wrapping around Diesel's side. Nails tore through his gear and into flesh. He gasped, blood pooling beneath him.

Jonah raised his rifle, but Wildcat was already moving.

Her SCAR-H thundered. Rounds slammed into the creature's ribs. The hits rocked it, but it clung tight.

Diesel's breath came in ragged gasps as the pressure increased.

Valkyrie rushed in. She grabbed Diesel's vest and yanked hard. His body jerked as the nails tore free. Blood poured from the wound, but he was clear.

Jonah and Wildcat fired together.

The Sasquatch's head snapped back as bullets punched through its skull. It dropped beside Diesel's crumpled body.

"Get him to the boat!" Jonah shouted.

Rook and Wildcat pulled Diesel up, dragging him toward the dock. Blood streamed behind them.

Alongside them, Havoc screamed at Rob to move faster.

A blur cut from the trees.

Valkyrie vanished.

The creature had come from her blind side. It snatched her clean off her feet and disappeared into the forest. Her SCAR-H hit the ground behind her.

"Valkyrie!" Breaker shouted, skidding to a halt.

Whisper's voice snapped through comms. "She's down! East side. Taken into the trees! I didn't see it!"

Jonah didn't stop.

"No one splits! We lose the team, we all die!"

But inside, everything in him screamed to go after her.

****

Valkyrie couldn't breathe. The creature held her under one thick, matted arm. Its leathery hide crushed into her ribs. The stench was overwhelming—wet hair, rotted meat, and something a whole lot worse.

Branches whipped her face. Thorns tore at her arms. A branch sliced her cheek.

She kicked and twisted, but it didn't matter. The thing's grip was unbreakable. Her ribs ached. Her chest felt like it was folding in.

Her hand found the FNX-45 Tactical on her hip.

She couldn't aim. But she didn't need to.

The creature let out a deep, rumbling growl, like gravel grinding in its throat.

She felt its pace slow slightly as it angled toward deeper trees.

Now.

She twisted just enough to jam the barrel downward. She fired once. The shot tore into its groin.

The beast shrieked, a wet, gurgling sound unlike

anything human. It buckled but didn't drop her.

She fired again. And again. Blood sprayed her gloves and face.

The Sasquatch screamed, its grip convulsing and loosening. It dropped her like dead weight, doubled over, and slammed face-first into the forest floor.

It howled, hands grasping at the ruin between its legs.

Valkyrie hit the ground hard. Her knees buckled. Her shoulder slammed into a rock. Stars flashed across her vision.

She staggered up and ran.

The woods ripped at her as she sprinted. Every breath hurt. Every step jostled bruises.

Behind her, it howled in agony.

Whisper's voice snapped through her earpiece. "I've got you. You're a hundred yards from the shore. Clearing due west. Veer left."

She pivoted.

Moonlight flickered through the trees.

Fifty yards.

Her lungs screamed, but she kept moving.

Whisper again.

"One on your ass. Big female. Move faster."

Valkyrie didn't look back. She didn't need to. She could hear it. The crashing of brush. The snapping of wood. It was close.

She burst out of the trees.

The boat was there, docked and ready. The rest of Echo Black was already loading in.

The lake shimmered in moonlight.

"She's coming. Thirty-five yards," Whisper said.

Valkyrie hit the dock. The boards groaned under her weight.

Behind her, another crack. Louder.

The Sasquatch had reached the dock.

Thudding steps pounded closer.

Twenty yards to the boat.

Jonah stood at the stern, rifle raised. Reaper just behind him, already sighting in.

"Move!" Jonah shouted.

Valkyrie sprinted.

The dock groaned again. A crack. Then it shattered.

The Sasquatch's weight proved too much. The dock exploded beneath her. She crashed through, screeching.

The water wasn't deep, but it was enough.

Valkyrie dove into the boat. Rook grabbed her and pulled her in.

The Sasquatch surged up from the water, howling.

Jonah fired.

One round took her in the temple.

The second made sure.

She fell back into the lake, half-submerged. Blood bloomed in the water.

On the shoreline, movement. More shapes breaking through the treeline.

A cluster of Sasquatch ran along the shore, moving with speed. Four of them. Maybe five. Closing in fast from Echo Black's blind side.

Breaker saw them.

He was already loading a 40mm HE round into his M320 launcher, mounted beneath his SCAR-H.

He snapped it shut with a click.

"A little parting gift."

He stepped to the edge of the stern, aimed toward the line of charging shapes, and fired.

The grenade arced across the water and landed just ahead of the oncoming horde.

The detonation lit the shoreline in orange fire.

Dirt and flame erupted. One of the Sasquatch vanished in the blast. Another was thrown sideways, skidding across the rocks. The others staggered, limbs torn, shrieking in rage and pain.

Smoke curled off the burning underbrush.

The immediate threat was gone.

Breaker glanced toward Valkyrie, who was slumped beside the railing, sore and breathless.

"You good?" Wildcat asked, crouched beside her.

Valkyrie nodded weakly. "Shot it in the dick."

Breaker let out a laugh, half-strangled and raw. "Hell yeah, you did."

Jonah gave her a nod, silent and proud.

Breaker moved to the cleat and ripped the mooring line free.

"We are not dying at the goddamn dock!"

He tossed the rope aside.

"Clear! Go! Go! Go!"

Whisper hit the throttle.

The boat surged forward, slicing through the lake. Wind tore past them, engine roaring.

Shapes moved in the trees behind them.

More howls. More rage.

Whisper stood at the console for only a moment before

Breaker slid in beside him.

"I've got it," Breaker said, gripping the wheel. "Eyes up, tech wizard."

Whisper nodded, already stepping away and flipping open his tablet.

On the shore, the remaining Sasquatch stood, watching them go.

CHAPTER 32

The boat surged toward the far shore, the engine's growl cutting through the eerie silence.

Jonah's eyes locked on their vehicles, parked near the water, positioned for a fast escape. The forest beyond them remained still, too still.

Beside him, Whisper tensed.

"Two incoming, 2 o'clock," he said.

Jonah saw them a second later.

Two massive Sasquatch burst from the treeline, running full-speed toward the vehicles.

Jonah's rounds ripped through the air, but the creatures were too fast.

Their enormous bodies moved like blurs in the moonlight, dodging between the bullets.

A shot clipped one in the side, but it didn't stop.

The first Sasquatch slammed into the nearest Suburban with a thunderous crack.

The second beast followed, its hulking shoulder colliding with the vehicle's frame.

Metal screamed. The SUV lurched sideways, teetering, then toppled over, smashing onto its side, pulling the trailer with it.

Glass shattered. Dust and debris filled the air.

Jonah gritted his teeth. They had just lost a vehicle.

The Sasquatch turned, snarling, and this time, they weren't fast enough.

Havoc moved to the front of the boat, crouching beside Jonah.

Without a word, he raised his Knight's Armament LAMG and opened fire.

Together, they unleashed hell.

Jonah's SCAR-H barked in tight bursts, hammering the lead creature's torso.

His rounds tore through thick hide and muscle, punching deep into the beast's chest.

It howled, staggering, its enormous arms clawing at the air as it collapsed.

Havoc's armor-piercing belt rounds carved through the second creature's throat, shredding flesh and bone.

Jonah adjusted his aim and fired again as it fell to the ground.

The round struck just below its eye.

It twitched once and fell still.

The boat crunched into the shallows, its hull grinding over wet sand.

They were in.

"Go, go!" Jonah barked.

Breaker jumped out first, rifle up. He moved quickly, sweeping the area. Jonah followed, boots sinking into the damp ground, then Whisper.

Havoc and Reaper pulled Diesel out next. He gritted his teeth, barely holding in a groan as they hauled him onto solid ground. Blood still seeped from his hastily applied bandages, but he stayed conscious.

Rob was next. He didn't have the strength to stand on his own, so Rook and Wildcat lifted him out carefully, supporting his weight.

Jonah and Breaker remained outside, scanning the treeline for any sign of movement while the others helped each other into the Suburban.

With no time to argue over comfort, four of them piled into the back, wedged between gear and drone cases.

Jonah waited until the last person was in before finally jumping into the passenger seat.

Havoc slammed the gas. The Suburban kicked up sand, spinning before catching traction and launching forward.

Jonah took one last glance in the side mirror.

The overturned Suburban sat in the darkness, the dead sasquatch sprawled around it.

Nothing moved.

CHAPTER 33

ECHO BLACK

The Suburban roared down the gravel road, tires kicking up loose rock behind them. Even with the headlights piercing the darkness, the forest felt suffocating and unending.

Inside, everyone was crammed together, weapons pressing awkwardly against ribs and legs. Diesel leaned against the door, pale, and sweating, Valkyrie keeping pressure on his wounds. Rob sat hunched near the backseat, still wrapped in the blanket someone had given him, his body stiff from exhaustion and exposure.

Havoc kept his eyes on the road, watching both the winding path ahead and the treeline. He expected movement. A flash of hair. A blur of motion. Something to explode from the trees at any second.

But for now, the forest was still.

The inside of the vehicle was quiet, too. No one spoke.

They were all still processing.

The gunfire. The chase. The bodies hitting the dirt. The sheer, unrelenting violence of it all.

Rob shifted slightly under the blanket. His throat was still raw, his limbs weak, but he forced himself to speak.

"…How did you know I was still alive?"

Jonah didn't look back. "We asked Levi."

Rob stiffened.

Jonah continued, his voice level. "We asked if anyone could have made it. He said only you."

Rob gripped the blanket tighter. Something inside him cracked open, a relief so sharp it almost hurt.

Levi was alive.

The last time he had seen him, Levi stood helpless as Rob was dragged into the forest.

His chest rose and fell in slow, steady breaths. He swallowed hard, his voice quieter now.

"…Is he okay?"

Valkyrie, still keeping pressure on Diesel's wounds, glanced over at him. "Physically? Yeah. He's out of the hospital." She exhaled deeply. "Mentally? Doubt it."

Rob nodded slightly. He understood. No one came out of something like this unscathed.

His mouth opened slowly, his jaw trembling as he struggled to form the words.

"W…were the others… found?" he asked, the sentence catching awkwardly in his throat.

Valkyrie glanced at him, her voice flat. "No."

Rob gazed out the window, his heart heavy.

The Suburban sped forward, the gravel road stretching ahead.

Finally, after what felt like forever, the rough, uneven terrain smoothed out. They hit pavement.

They were officially on the highway, heading south toward Duluth.

In the back, Whisper shifted slightly. As he did, his phone vibrated against his vest.

Instinctively, he reached for it.

"Hold up," he said as he tried to free his arm. Rook, sitting beside him, adjusted his position so he could move.

Whisper pulled the phone from his vest, glancing at the screen.

His entire body went still.

Then, in a flat voice, he said, "We've got a problem."

Jonah, still watching the road, didn't turn. "What?"

Whisper turned the screen toward him.

It was a live feed from the cabin's security cameras.

The grainy night-vision footage showed large, hulking shapes moving through the property.

The cabin was under siege.

Sasquatch crashed onto the porch, ripping through the railing like twigs. One of the cameras shook violently, the feed distorting, as something massive struck it.

One of them tore the front door clean off its hinges and flung it into the trees.

"They found the cabin," Whisper said.

Breaker let out a slow exhale. "Well. Good thing we didn't go there first."

No one argued.

In the passenger seat, Jonah pulled out his phone. His fingers moved quickly over the screen.

We got him. He's alive.

He hit send, then locked the screen and slipped the phone back into his pocket.

The Suburban sped to the hospital, the ruined cabin now nothing more than a problem for another day.

CHAPTER 34

THE SANCTUARY

The cold water lapped gently at the edges of the creek, fed by an underground spring. The moon's reflection shimmered on the surface, disturbed only by the ripples of two colossal figures stepping into the shallows.

Aluk and Matto crouched low, scooping up handfuls of water. Blood swirled into the current before vanishing downstream.

Aluk drank deeply, his chest vibrating with a deep grunt of satisfaction. Matto did the same, though his movements were slower, more careful.

No croaks from the reeds, no rustling in the underbrush. Any creature within miles had gone silent, driven into hiding by the chaos.

A long breath escaped Matto's lips, visible in the cold morning air. He turned his head toward Aluk, letting out a low, layered grunt.

"The clan will mourn for many nights."

Aluk did not answer immediately. He ran a thick hand over his wounded shoulder, where Reaper's round had torn through flesh and muscle. The skin was raw and split, dark blood caked along his upper arm and collarbone. His hip ached where another round had struck, and his left side throbbed with every movement. Beneath it all, the blistered skin across his back and neck still burned from the earlier grenade blast.

Another throb pulsed through his jaw, deep and grinding. The bullet had torn through his cheek and shattered part of his jaw, taking several teeth with it. Blood still wept from the ragged hole, a slow, steady ooze that ran along his chin. Half his ear was gone, and the side of his face was crusted with blood, still wet in places, the wound swollen and raw.

Matto was watching him, waiting.

Aluk finally lifted his chin and exhaled a grunt of dismissal.

"Let them mourn. We are still strong."

Matto's brow lowered, but he didn't respond. Instead, he laid back into the cool water, letting it soothe the singed skin along his back.

Aluk followed, immersing his arms and shoulders beneath the surface. The water stung, but it was cleansing. Necessary.

Matto let out a series of jagged grunts.

"Why did you not follow the hairless ones?"

Aluk took his time to reply, then answered in a low, gravelly rumble.

"Not right time."

Matto said nothing more. They stood in silence, then stepped out of the creek, water dripping from their huge frames. Mist clung to their skin as they began the slow walk home.

****

The first light of dawn crept through the trees, revealing the devastation left behind.

Aluk moved forward with purpose, his gaze fixed ahead, never wavering.

But Matto couldn't look away.

The bodies of their fallen littered the ground, twisted and broken. Some had been torn apart, their insides exposed to the cold morning air. Others lay in unnatural positions, limbs bent at odd angles, faces frozen in expressions of pain.

A deep exhale left Matto's chest as he slowed his steps.

A warrior he had hunted alongside lay motionless against a fallen log, his red-amber eyes open but unseeing. The female beside him had been struck with such force that her chest had caved inward, ribs splintering like broken branches.

Matto let out a low, mournful grunt, his fingers twitching at his sides.

He glanced toward Aluk, waiting for some acknowledgment.

But Aluk never turned his head.

He stepped over bodies without hesitation, his pace steady.

Behind them, the remainder of the clan moved through the trees in near silence, carrying the last of the bodies back to the sanctuary. One by one, the fallen were lifted with reverence and care. No cries of grief. No wails. Only the sound of bodies being returned to their home.

They would be prepared for burial inside the cave, each one laid to rest beneath the stone, in the place of their ancestors.

Matto gritted his teeth. His grief simmered just beneath the surface, a burn behind his eyes he refused to let fall.

But Aluk kept walking.

Matto lingered for a moment longer before forcing himself to move. His pace slowed; his breaths were deep and labored.

When they reached the clearing of the sanctuary, what remained of the clan was already gathered.

The Elder stood at the mouth of the cave, his bulky frame rigid, illuminated by the glow of the rising sun.

His red-amber eyes burned like embers as he fixed them on Aluk.

The others had felt their approach. Warriors, females and younglings alike had formed a wide, tense circle around the cave entrance. Most were wounded, but they were standing, waiting.

A soft, keening sound carried through the clearing, one of the females mourning beside her fallen mate.

But all eyes were on Aluk.

The Elder took a slow breath, releasing it in a deep, reverberating grunt.

A warning.

A demand for submission.

Aluk did not kneel.

Matto hesitated for a brief moment before slowly stepping away, placing himself among the others.

He knew what was coming.

The Elder grunted, a sharp command, his hand gesturing towards the fallen bodies.

"I warned you. You bring this death."

Aluk stood firm.

The Elder took a step forward, his oversized hands curling into fists.

His next grunt was deeper, layered with anger and grief.

"The clan mourns, and you bring only war."

A ripple of unease spread through the gathered Sasquatch.

Aluk's chest rumbled with a steady, unyielding sound. His eyes locked onto the Elder's, unblinking.

The Elder's lips pulled back slightly, his burning eyes narrowing. He let out a ragged grunt, the sound biting like the snap of a branch.

"Fools die because of your vengeance."

Aluk flexed his fingers, lifting his chin slightly. His posture remained rigid, defiant.

His answer came as a rolling series of grunts, firm and unshaken.

"The hairless ones take what is ours. They burn our land. Hunt our food. I warned you the old ways were over."

The Elder exhaled sharply, his gaze darkening.

His next grunt was slow, controlled.

"No, Aluk. This is your doing."

Aluk's breath came hard and hot.

The Elder stepped closer, his presence pressing into the space between them.

"You have doomed us all."

Aluk tensed up. His breath deepened, his muscles flexing beneath his skin.

He had heard enough.

With a raw, snarling bellow, he attacked.

CHAPTER 35

THE SANCTUARY

The Elder was ready for Aluk.

The younger beast ran, his feet tearing through the dirt as he barreled toward the Elder. His fists swung in a blur, aiming for the throat, the skull, anywhere that would bring the old one down fast.

He twisted to the side, Aluk's first strike grazing past his shoulder. The second, aimed at his ribs, was caught mid-air. The Elder's fingers wrapped around Aluk's forearm, his grip like stone.

Then he struck back.

A powerful fist slammed into Aluk's head, sending him stumbling. His ears rang, vision flashing with spots, but he didn't fall.

The Elder was already moving again, stepping in to press the attack.

Aluk recovered fast. He ducked under the Elder's next swing and surged forward, ramming his shoulder into the older warrior's chest. The impact sent both of them staggering through the clearing.

The clan moved back, giving them space.

A deep, rhythmic grunting rippled through the gathered Sasquatch, some urging Aluk on, others calling for the Elder to finish it.

Matto watched from the edge of the circle.

The Elder let out a low, grunting breath as he stood tall, his chest expanded rapidly.

"You are reckless. You waste lives."

With bared teeth, Aluk stared at the Elder from under his brow. His grunts were heavy, splitting the air.

"They will be replaced. More of our kind will come."

The Elder's face hardened. His eyes flicked to the bodies of the fallen, then back to Aluk. His next grunt came slow, weighted.

"They were your family."

Aluk roared and charged again.

This time, the Elder didn't sidestep. He met the attack head-on.

They collided with a force that sent tremors through the ground.

Hulking arms locked around each other, muscles straining, feet digging into the dirt as each tried to overpower the other. Aluk was younger, stronger, but the Elder had fought more battles than any of them. He knew how to use his weight, his experience.

Suddenly, the Elder snapped his head forward and delivered a brutal headbutt.

The sound was sharp, a bone-on-bone crack that echoed through the clearing. The impact rattled both of them—Aluk stumbled, momentarily dazed, and even the Elder staggered, blood trickling down from a split above his brow.

But it broke the momentum.

Snarling, Aluk twisted hard, using the Elder's own weight against him. The shift sent them both tumbling. They hit the ground hard, rolling through the dirt in a blur of limbs and fists.

Aluk came out on top.

He drove his fist into the Elder's face, a heavy, bone-crunching blow.

The Elder grunted but did not go still. His legs kicked up, knees slamming into Aluk's ribs, sending him sprawling to the side.

Both of them scrambled to their feet, panting.

A circle of watching eyes burned into them.

The Elder's breath was deep, controlled. His arms hung loose but ready, body shifting as he adjusted his footing.

Aluk's chest heaved, his fingers flexing at his sides.

Matto saw the subtle change then. The Elder was tiring.

But so was Aluk.

And Aluk knew it.

The Elder stood tall, warm blood dripped from his face.

Aluk rolled his shoulders, shaking out his limbs, his muscles burning from the exertion of the fight. He had the advantage of youth, size and strength, but the Elder had endured far worse battles. He had ruled long before Aluk had taken his first steps, guiding the clan through harsh winters and wars with rival clans.

But that time was long gone.

The clan had gathered close, their once-rousing grunts of encouragement now faded into a watchful silence. Some warriors had stepped forward, forming a loose circle, their eyes flicking between the two combatants. They knew this was not just a fight, it was a reckoning.

The small sasquatch that had befriended Rob, peeked out from behind one of the females, his small frame hunched, his breath barely audible. His wide amber eyes darted between Aluk and the Elder, unblinking. He had never seen anything like this before.

Matto stood nearby, his nostrils flaring as he inhaled deep, fast breaths. This fight had already gone too far.

Aluk lifted his chin, baring his teeth in a slow, deliberate show of dominance. His deep, commanding grunts rumbled through his chest, shaking the surrounding air.

"The hairless ones have taken too much. Stolen too much. And you…" he let the word hang, an ungodly growl lacing his grunts, *"have done nothing."*

The Elder did not react. His eyes remained fixed on Aluk, watching.

Aluk let out short, harsh grunts, stepping closer. Never taking his eyes off the Elder.

"You let the hairless ones walk our ground. You let them take water, trees, meat." His grunts came fast, rough. *"We watched. We waited. That was the old way."*

He slammed a fist against his own chest, the sound deep and resonant.

"I do not wait. I do not kneel. We will go take what's theirs."

A murmur of low chatter rippled through the watching warriors. Some nodded. Others remained still, waiting for the Elder to respond.

The Elder's gaze did not waver, though his shoulders squared. His grunts came slow. *"You bring war too soon. You bring thunder to our home. To our young."*

He stepped closer, voice deepening. *"Their blood is on you. You brought the hairless one. You knew the others would follow."*

Aluk's nostrils flared. *"War was already here. The hairless ones have made it so."*

He turned, gesturing toward the scattered bodies of their

fallen. Their lifeless forms lay in the dirt, their hair matted with blood, their bodies broken by the thunder sticks of the hairless ones.

The Elder's gaze flickered to the bodies, his brow lowering. He did not need to be reminded of the loss. *"You made it so,"* he grunted.

Aluk saw the hesitation. He pressed forward, his voice a low, rolling growl. *"You kept us in the shadows. Hiding. Running. But I will not hide."* He stood eye to eye with the Elder. *"I will send for the others. They will fight with us. We will end them before they return with more thunder sticks."*

A few warriors grunted their approval.

Matto stiffened. *"If the hairless ones come in greater numbers, you will lead us to ruin,"* he growled under his breath, but Aluk ignored him.

The Elder's shoulders tensed. His grunts came heavier now, more forceful. *"You are blinded by rage. You would risk everything for vengeance. That is not strength."*

Air hissed through Aluk's nose, his breath coming faster. He could feel the shift now, the unspoken challenge between them thick in the air.

The Elder took a step closer. *"Strength is knowing when to* act. *Knowing when to wait."*

Aluk's growl deepened, a low, dangerous rumble. *"That is weakness."*

The Elder's eyes flickered with something unreadable.

Aluk struck first.

He lunged, his massive arms swinging in a brutal arc. The Elder anticipated it, sidestepping in a blur of motion He brought his elbow up, slamming it into the side of Aluk's skull. The impact sent a sharp jolt through Aluk's body, his vision flashing white.

He stumbled but recovered quickly, shaking his head.

The Elder pressed the advantage, driving forward. His fists came fast, striking Aluk's ribs, his jaw, his stomach. Each hit carried the power of a warrior who had fought through decades of battles.

But Aluk was faster.

He twisted, catching the Elder's arm mid-swing and wrenching it hard. A sickening crack echoed through the clearing as he drove his knee into the Elder's chest, sending him sprawling into the dirt.

The watching warriors grunted, some in approval,

others in unease.

The Elder coughed, spitting blood onto the ground. But he did not stay down. He pushed himself up, his arms trembling slightly, but his gaze was still intense.

Aluk charged.

He feinted left before slamming his fist into the Elder's ribs, then followed it with a vicious strike to the jaw. The Elder reeled, stumbling.

Matto shifted uneasily.

For the first time, the Elder looked unsteady.

Aluk saw it.

And he did not stop.

He struck again. And again.

A backhand sent the Elder staggering, and before he could regain his footing, Aluk's huge hands closed around his throat.

Matto tensed, knowing Aluk would not stop.

The Elder's eyes met Aluk's.

There was no plea. No fear.

Only resignation.

Then his gaze flickered over Aluk's face.

The wound.

A black, blood-crusted gash where the bullet had torn through flesh.

The Elder grunted low in his throat.

Aluk's stance shifted, sensing something, but too late.

The Elder sprang—not at Aluk's throat, not at his ribs, but at the jagged wound.

His fingers dug into the torn flesh, pressing hard.

Aluk let out a roar of pain, his vision flashing white-hot. His legs nearly buckled as agony ripped through him.

The Elder held on, his grip cruel and unrelenting, twisting his fingers deeper into the wound.

Aluk lashed out, driving his fist into the side of the Elder's skull. The old warrior's body jerked from the impact, but he did not release his grip.

Another blow.

Then another.

The Elder's hands finally slipped.

Aluk staggered back, panting, blood spilling fresh onto the dirt. The wound had been ripped wide open, raw, ragged, and nearly double in size.

The Elder tried to rise.

Aluk's hand shot out, wrapping around his throat.

Matto took another step forward, eyes wide, but he did not interfere. It would be a death sentence.

The Elder's breath came in deep, wheezing pulls. His fingers curled, then went slack.

Aluk squeezed.

The Elder's throat gave a wet, sickening crunch.

Matto turned his head just before the sound of snapping bone broke the silence.

The Elder's body crumpled, lifeless, hitting the ground with a loud thump.

A wave of hushed, uneasy grunts moved through the clan.

Blood dripped from Aluk's fingers.

The young sasquatch remained near the females, his wide eyes locked on the fallen Elder.

Aluk stood over the Elder's body, his breath deep and steady. Blood ran down his face and throat, dripping onto the dirt beside the motionless form. He lifted his chin, staring down at the fallen leader.

Then he threw back his head and roared.

The sound was primal, echoing through the clearing like a thunderclap, raw, savage, and victorious. Trees shuddered with the force of it, and the clan felt it in their bones.

He turned to face them, his chest heaving, eyes blazing.

With a series of grunts, his voice rumbled across the clearing, layered with finality.

"The old ways die with him."

The gathered Sasquatch shifted, their eyes locked on Aluk, absorbing the meaning behind his words.

Aluk's bloodied knuckles flexed as he let out another low, commanding string of grunts.

"Now, we take what is theirs."

A deep, resounding growl spread through the warriors.

Some beat their chests. Others bared their teeth, the fire in their eyes reflecting the dawn's first light.

They would take the war to the hairless ones.

EPILOGUE

DULUTH, MINNESOTA

The hospital bustled with quiet urgency. Rushed footsteps, clipped voices, the occasional squeak of a gurney wheel. Nurses passed in and out of rooms speaking in low tones.

Rob lay beneath a thick layer of hospital blankets, his skin scratched and pale, his lips cracked. An IV ran into the crook of his arm, slowly delivering fluids and nutrients back into his system. A nasal cannula fed warm oxygen into his lungs. The warmth of the hospital room was a far cry from the freezing hell he had barely escaped.

Outside the window, snow flurried gently across the Duluth skyline. But in here, it was still. Quiet.

He was alive.

It had been touch and go when Echo Black got him onto the boat. He had been barely conscious by the time they got to the hospital, his skin ice-cold to the touch. Core temperature in the danger zone. Heartbeat weak. Dehydrated. Starved. His muscles had begun to break down—early signs of rhabdomyolysis from prolonged exposure and physical trauma. His kidneys had nearly shut down.

But he had made it.

And now, days later, he lay in a clean hospital bed, color slowly returning to his skin.

His mother sat at his bedside, holding his hand with both of hers. His father stood at the foot of the bed, silent, his eyes fixed on his son's face. His younger sister, curled into the armchair, had fallen asleep sometime in the morning, her jacket still wrapped tightly around her.

They hadn't left since he'd been brought in.

When Rob stirred, blinking slowly against the light streaming in through the window, the tension shattered like glass.

"Rob?" his mother whispered, leaning in.

His dry lips cracked as he tried to speak. Nothing came

out but a wheeze.

He blinked.

A tear rolled down his mother's cheek. "You're safe now. You're going to be okay."

They had mourned for him.

And somehow, Echo Black had gotten him home.

Rob's mind was foggy, but fragments flickered in and out. Trees. Teeth. Screams. Cold. And then warmth. A woman's voice. Valkyrie. The lake.

The memory of Tyson's windbreaker clenched in his hands.

But now, for the first time in what felt like forever, his heart didn't race. His limbs weren't frozen stiff. He wasn't bound to a tree, unable to stop his body from shaking. He wasn't staring into the eyes of something ancient and furious. He was here.

The IV in his arm delivered warm fluids into his dehydrated veins. He could feel them, not painful, not uncomfortable, just there. A quiet lifeline. He was wrapped in blankets, a cocoon of clean linen and human care. Machines monitored everything, his heart, his breathing, the oxygen in his blood.

His chest ached when he breathed, not from injury, but from the heaviness of everything that had happened. From the knowledge that others hadn't made it out. The faces of his friends drifted into his mind, laughing at the campfire, fighting with Carter before he stormed off and never returning. Bree.

He blinked hard, trying to push their faces from his mind.

But one image refused to leave.

The young Sasquatch.

The memory of those glowing amber eyes, wide and uncertain. The hesitant grunts. The water bottle. The berries. The windbreaker.

That Sasquatch had saved his life.

He hadn't understood why. Maybe he never would. But the creature had brought him food, warmth and just enough hope to survive one more night. One more hour. One more breath.

Was the copper one still alive? Had it made it through the fight? Or had the chaos taken it too?

The thought sat heavy in his chest.

He didn't know how long he lay there like that, thinking of the copper one, the others, the sanctuary, the chase through the forest. But eventually, the door creaked open.

A nurse stepped in quietly, her voice warm but professional. "Hey there, sunshine. Let's check your vitals, hmm?"

She leaned down and checked the nasal cannula, making sure it was secure as warm oxygen flowed into his lungs. The world felt a little closer now, the sterile air cool against his skin. She checked his heart rate, oxygen and blood pressure, then adjusted the flow on his IV and smiled as she met his eyes.

"You're severely dehydrated," the nurse said gently, checking the monitor. "You've got bruised ribs, signs of exposure, frostbite on a few toes, but nothing we can't treat. You're strong."

Rob tried to speak. His throat creaked, dry and raw. He cleared it with effort, then managed a hoarse, "Thank you."

The nurse gave him a gentle pat on the arm and slipped out of the room, pulling the door halfway closed behind her.

Not five seconds later, it opened again.

Levi opened the door slowly, his knit beanie in one hand. When his eyes landed on Rob, a smile spread across his face. Pure relief.

His eyes scanned Rob from head to toe, taking in the scratches and the ghost-pale skin.

Then, with a smirk, he said, "Jesus, you look like hell."

Rob's lips cracked into the faintest smile. His voice was hoarse, but it came out just loud enough.

"Feel worse."

Levi stepped into the room, slowly. He looked tired but relieved.

He gave a small nod to Rob's mother and father in acknowledgment, then crossed the room and grabbed a spare chair. The legs scraped lightly against the tile as he pulled it up beside the bed.

Rob didn't flinch. He was too tired.

Levi sat and studied Rob for a moment, the exhaustion plain on his face.

He let out a deep breath. "Thought we lost you, man." Rob nodded, his exhaustion evident in the dark circles under his eyes. "Me too."

A quiet moment passed. Then Rob's father stepped forward and placed a hand on Levi's back.

"Thank you," he said softly. "If you hadn't informed that team Rob might still be alive, if you hadn't told them where to look… we wouldn't have our son back."

Levi shook his head slightly. "Thank you, but it was all on Rob and the team. I just pointed them in the right direction."

Rob smiled slightly, grateful to see his friend again.

Then he paused. His brow pinched slightly and he turned his head toward his mother.

"The jacket," he said, his voice rough. "The windbreaker… the one I was wearing. Where is it?"

She blinked, caught off guard. "They gave it to us. It's at home. It smelled horribly so I washed it."

He let out a breath. It sounded like relief.

"Good," he whispered. "I want to give it to Tyson's parents."

His mother's eyes softened. She reached for his hand and gave it a light squeeze.

Levi didn't speak right away. But the look he gave Rob

said plenty.

He was proud of him. And grateful he was still here.

Alive.

Safe.

ABOUT THE AUTHOR

 Luka T. Jacobs, an author from the picturesque Illawarra region south of Sydney, Australia, is passionate about cryptids like Sasquatch and Dogman. She lives there with her partner and their dog, Finnigan.

Luka's love for animals and adventure fuels her storytelling. With a background in Graphic Design and Art, she adds a unique visual flair to her work. An avid traveler and explorer, she draws inspiration from the wild, eager to share her imaginative worlds with readers.

Luka T. Jacobs

Stay connected and join the conversation!

FB: https://www.facebook.com/lukatjacobs
A: https://amazon.com/author/lukatjacobs
W: http://www.LukaTJacobs.com

JOIN CRYPTID HORROR CENTRAL

Join my email list and get first access to new releases and download my **FREE** short story *"The Dogman of Coldwater Creek"*.

W W W . L U K A T J A C O B S . C O M

Dear Reader,

Thank you for choosing my book amidst a sea of choices—
it truly means the world to me.

If you enjoyed the story, I'd love it if you shared
your experience with others and left a review.
As an independent author, your voice helps bring
these tales to life for more readers, and every
recommendation makes a tremendous impact.

Thank you again for joining me on this journey.
I'm so grateful to have you as a reader!

SNEAK PEEK:

WATCHTOWER RECKONING: SASQUATCH AWAKENING

Buckley Jones slammed the flimsy back door behind him for the fifth time this week. Remarkably, despite its precarious hold on the hinges, the door remained intact. Known to the townsfolk simply as Buck, he was a figure more often avoided than approached, his temperamental nature and penchant for trouble leaving many wary of crossing his path.

The source of today's argument with his wife was a familiar one, Buck's relentless drinking, which had now devoured the last remnants of their government assistance check. With a cigarette dangling between his fingers, Buck sought respite in the haze of smoke, eager to distance himself from the incessant nagging of his wife. This brief escape into the nicotine cloud offered a momentary reprieve from the escalating strife that had, yet again, engulfed his home.

Mumbling to himself about the perpetual misfortunes of his life, Buck lamented how everything, including life itself, had always been crap to him. He railed against his wife, branding her a 'miserable old sod' under his breath. In his embittered monologue, Buck's words were laced with venom and defeat, a reflection of a life marred by regret and misplaced anger.

He settled into the worn chair on his porch, the cigarette smoke curling lazily around him. As he brooded over his misfortunes, a twig snapped in the forest behind his home, shattering the eerie silence of the night. Buck's head snapped up, his senses on high alert.

With his false bravado, he called out, "Who's there?" His voice wavered slightly, betraying the underlying fear that churned within him. When no reply came, he rose from his seat, the adrenaline coursing through his veins.

"Show yourselves!" he bellowed, his voice echoing into the darkness. "I'm armed, and I ain't afraid to use it!" But the forest remained silent, its secrets cloaked in shadow.

After a tense moment, Buck hesitated, his bravado waning in the face of the unknown. With a nervous glance over his shoulder, he retreated to his chair, the sense of foreboding lingering in the surrounding air.

Buck's mumbling ceased abruptly when he noticed the eerie quiet around him. This silence, profound and unsettling, lacked the usual cacophony of insects—a stark absence that made it seem as if nature itself had recoiled in anticipation of what was to come.

Deep in the pit of his stomach, Buck knew something wasn't right and suddenly felt immense dread. He had neglected to switch on the porch light upon stepping out, relying instead on the moonlight that typically bathed his backyard.

Then, from right behind him came a growl so deep and menacing it seemed to echo from the depths of a nightmare. The sound, imbued with an evil intent, was enough to still Buck's heart. He could feel the hot breath of whatever was growling. Paralyzed with fear, he could not muster the courage to turn and face the source of the sound.

A sense of unease gnawed at Buck's insides, an intuitive warning that something was terribly wrong, blossoming into a suffocating dread. Overwhelmed by terror, Buck felt a warm liquid spreading over his jeans.

In that moment of utter fear, Buck—a man defined by a life of hardship and anger—found himself whispering prayers into the encroaching darkness, desperately seeking salvation from the looming threat.

Yet, no divine intervention came to Buck's aid. The Sasquatch, fueled by primal rage, executed a swift and brutal judgment. With terrifying ease, the creature placed each of its hands on the sides of Buck's head. In one swift, brutal motion, it tore his head clean off and hurled it against the side of the house, a gruesome testament to the creature's immense strength.

This act of savagery marked the end of Buck's turbulent journey, a life extinguished as suddenly as it had been lived.

Meanwhile, inside their home, Vera's startled voice pierced the chaos. "What was that racket, Buck?" she called out, unaware of the horror unfolding just beyond their door.

Hearing Vera's voice, the enraged Sasquatch redirected its malevolent fury towards the house. It crashed through the back door with unbridled force, shattering the once-peaceful night with a cacophony of destruction and terror. Thus began a nightmare that would soon engulf the entire town, its residents caught in a relentless tide of violence and fear.

★ ★ ★ ★ ★

"Luka T. Jacobs' nightmare scenario is entertaining and suspenseful. It made me never want to go vacationing in small towns (especially near the woods).

The Sasquatch(es) are not just rampaging monsters. Some of the story is actually from their perspective and allow readers to understand the motivations behind their hatred of humans. Lots of action, Bigfoot carnage, and even a surprisingly strong tale of friendship among the main human characters. Great read. Looking forward to reading more of Luka's Bigfoot-related books. Highly recommend it!

O. QUIJADA, VERIFIED AMAZON PURCHASE

www.ingramcontent.com/pod-product-compliance
Lightning Source LLC
Chambersburg PA
CBHW071138180726
48291CB00007B/2235